HOW TO BE A SAINT

An Extremely Weird and Mildly Sacrilegious History of the Catholic Church's Biggest Names

Kate Sidley

For My Dad

Copyright © 2025 by Kate Sidley
Cover and internal design © 2025 by Sourcebooks
Cover and internal design by Lauren Smith and Jillian Rahn/Sourcebooks
Cover images © Francisco de Zurbarán, Saint Lucy, 1630, Hispanic Society of America/Public Domain, Francisco de Zurbarán, Saint Apollonia, 1636, Louvre Museum/Public Domain, Jacob Savery, Landscape with the story of Jephthah's daughter, 1580-1589, Rijksmuseum/Public Domain, Jean Bourdichon, Horae ad usum Parisiensem, dites Heures de Charles VIII, between circa 1475 and circa 1500, Bibliothèque nationale de France/Public Domain
Internal images © iii, Renata Sedmakova/Shutterstock; iv, Clemens Birsak/Adobe Stock; v, NPL - DeA Picture Library/Bridgeman Images; vi, 29, mikroman6/Getty Images; ix, bruce7/Getty Images; xi, 172, gldburger/Getty Images; xi, 4, 174, 175, xiii, ZU_09/Getty Images; xiv, PVDE/Bridgeman Images; xiv, duncan1890/Getty Images; xiv, Rouzes/Getty Images; xiv, woolwinephogotraphy/Getty Images; 2, 28, 170, Chorna Olena/Getty Images; 4, 11, 21, song_mi/Getty Images; 12, denisk0/Getty Images; 13, mikroman6/Getty Images; 15, ilbusca/Getty Images; 19, 46, 51, 52, 63, 66, 69, 89, 100, 101, Mykyta Dolmatov/Getty Images; 21, 33, AKO/Getty Images; 26, F. J. Carneros/Adobe Stock; 26, duncan1890/Getty Images; 26, maxstockphoto/Shutterstock; 29, milalala/Getty Images; 29, channarongsds/Getty Images; 33, NSA Digital Archive/Getty Images; 74, channarongsds/Getty Images; 165, johavel/Getty Images; 168, Keith Lance/Getty Images; 174, Dmitroscope/Getty Images; 174, Lazarev/Getty Images; 174, Dariia Karpova/Getty Images; 190, beinluck/Getty Images; 26, Francisco de Zurbarán, Saint Romanus of Antioch and Saint Barulas, 1638, Art Institute of Chicago/Public Domain; 168, Michelangelo, The Torment of Saint Anthony, 1487-88, Kimbell Art Museum/Public Domain; 3, 5, 9, 14, 16, 34, 36, 75, 80, 99, 102, 126, 130, 133, 135, 150, 152, 154, 190, 184, 187, kaer_istock/Getty Images

Sourcebooks and the colophon are registered trademarks of Sourcebooks.

All rights reserved. No part of this book may be reproduced in any form or by any electronic or mechanical means including information storage and retrieval systems—except in the case of brief quotations embodied in critical articles or reviews—without permission in writing from its publisher, Sourcebooks.

No part of this book may be used or reproduced in any manner for the purpose of training artificial intelligence technologies or systems.

This publication is designed to provide accurate and authoritative information in regard to the subject matter covered. It is sold with the understanding that the publisher is not engaged in rendering legal, accounting, or other professional service. If legal advice or other expert assistance is required, the services of a competent professional person should be sought. —*From a Declaration of Principles Jointly Adopted by a Committee of the American Bar Association and a Committee of Publishers and Associations*

This book is a work of humor and intended for entertainment purposes only.

All biblical verses are used as reflected in the New International Version (NIV) of the Christian Bible unless otherwise noted.

Published by Sourcebooks
P.O. Box 4410, Naperville, Illinois 60567-4410
(630) 961-3900
sourcebooks.com

Cataloging-in-Publication Data is on file with the Library of Congress.

Printed and bound in China.
TL 10 9 8 7 6 5 4 3 2 1

"To be a saint is not a privilege of a few…
All of us in baptism have the inheritance
of being able to become saints."
POPE FRANCIS

"You can do it. Put your back into it."
ICE CUBE

CONTENTS

Foreword by Stephen Colbert	vii
Welcome Letter from God	x
Holy FAQ!	xii

PART 1: How to Be a Catholic — 1
B.Y.O.B. (Bring Your Own Baptism)	5
The Basics	9
Anatomy of a Catholic	12
A Pope, by Any Other Name	14
The Bible Real Quick	16

PART 2: Sainthood in Five Easy-ish Steps — 27
Quiz: What Kind of Saint Are You?	30
An Introduction from Me, Saint Ulrich of Augsburg, the First Catholic Saint	34
Step 1: Die	36
Step 1: Checklist	40
Post-Death Options for Catholics	40
Is Martyrdom Right for Me?	42
Tips for the Aspiring Martyr	47
Saints Who Probably Joined Religious Orders Just to Avoid Shitty Marriages	50
Saints Who Are Sort of Like Zombies	55

Saints Who Were Virgins and Martyrs a.k.a. Virgin Martyrs	62
Saints Who Were Nepo Babies	67
Nepo Baby Saint Subcategory: Royalty	70
Step 1 Complete!	74
What the Hell Is a Halo?	75
Quick Halo Guide	78
Step 2: Have Your Whole Life Investigated	80
Step 2: Checklist	83
The Heroic Virtues	83
Quick Tips	86
Saints Who Could Kick Your Ass	87
Saints Who It Turns Out Probably Weren't Real	91
The Saint Sex Talk	93
Step 2 Complete!	98
Dress for the Job You Want	99
Step 3: Have Your Whole Life Investigated Again but by People in Rome This Time	102
Step 3: Checklist	106
"Money!"	106
Making a Saint Budget	109
Don't Beat Yourself Up. Or Maybe Do! Self-Mortification	110
Saints Who Did the Most	113
Saints Who Did the Bare Minimum	116
Saints Who Didn't Get Out Much	119
Step 3 Complete!	125
Patron Saints: Finding Your Thing	126
Can My Dog Be a Saint?	130
Saints Who Were Very Good Boys	133
Step 4: Do a Miracle	135
Step 4: Checklist	138
We Should Probably Pause Here to Mention That Some Saints Could Fly	138
Saints Who Could Do Cool Shit	142

Unclaimed Miracles	*147*
Step 4 Complete!	*149*
Make a Name for Yourself	**150**
Holy Nicknames	**152**
Step 5: Saint You!	**154**
Step 5: Checklist	*156*
You Want a Piece of Me? Relics!	*157*
Make Your Own Relic	*163*
Make Your Own Holy Card	*164*
Saints Who Walked Six Miles after Being Beheaded	*166*
Step 5 Complete!	*167*

PART 3: You're a Saint! Now What? — 169

Another Letter from God	**171**
Know Your Way around Heaven	**174**
City Saints, Country Saints	**176**
Saints You Can Eat	**180**
Saints Who Put the "Christ" Back in "Happy Holidays"	**184**
The Game of (After)Life	**187**
Certificate of Saintification	**190**

Quick Timeline of the History of Canonization	*191*
Glossary	*192*
Acknowledgments	*198*
Bibliography	*200*
About the Author	*210*

FOREWORD
by Stephen Colbert

> The only real sadness, the only real failure, the only great tragedy in life, is not to become a saint.
> **LEON BLOY, SAD FRENCH GUY**

Dear Reader/Sinner,

By picking up this book, you've already begun the long, sacred journey to sainthood. Or you just picked this up to buy time while you work up the courage to walk over to the fantasy elvish erotica novel you actually came here to buy. In which case, that guilt makes you an honorary Catholic. Welcome!

I've been Catholic for over sixty years, making me something of an expert. Church hierarchy goes: Pope, cardinals, bishops, famous comedians, priests, deacons, and last, the crucifix over your mom's kitchen sink that stares at you while you wash dishes. So it's with authority that I can say this is the best humor book about canonization I have ever read. It's also the only one, but let's focus on that first part.

As Catholics, we are taught to look to the saints for guidance on how to live virtuous lives. For example, my patron saint, Stephen, is known for being the first official martyr of Christianity. By standing up to the authorities, even at the cost of his own life, he inspires others to speak with courage and conviction. Plus, St. Stephen was stoned to death, so he's also who you pray to when you get WAY too high for the first time and think, *Oh no, am I going to feel like this forever?*

Being a Catholic isn't always easy. The rules can be complicated. The music is really hit or miss. The pews are uncomfortable. And the kneeling…so much uppin' and downin'. If God were truly merciful, our genuflection would consist of slowly tipping forward onto a bean bag chair.

Thankfully, Kate Sidley has written a book to make one of the most important, weirdest, and most obscure processes in Catholicism—canonization—a little bit easier.

Kate has written for me at *The Late Show* for years, and I can say with confidence that she is funny, intelligent, and absolutely not a saint. But she has read a lot about them. She's the perfect person to guide you through the canonization process (assuming no priests, nuns, scholars, or mall Santas were available). She has also assured me that this book is 100 percent guaranteed to get you into heaven or your money back. Just come back from the dead to tell Kate where you ended up, and she will personally cut you a fireproof check.

So I hope you enjoy *How to Be a Saint*. In fact, I hope you enjoy it so much that you buy copies for all of your friends and loved ones. My point is, I want you to buy the exact number of copies to send Kate's two children to college, but not so many that she stops working for me.

—Stephen Colbert

P. S. Now go enjoy your sexy elf book, ya nerdy freak.

WELCOME LETTER FROM GOD

Dear Prospective Saint,

Thank you for your interest in becoming a saint. It's an exciting time to be in heaven. Up here, there are infinite episodes of every reality show. You want season 10,476 of *Below Deck*? Done. We still have the original Four Loko and the never-released Seven Loko, which no mortal heart can handle. Plus, in heaven, your favorite jeans always fit. Feeling bloated? No, you're not. Boom. Heaven.

Let's get the awkward part out of the way first: yes, I am God. Yes, *that* God. The one from movies, TV, talk radio, country music, bumper stickers, acceptance speeches, and assorted swear words. You may know me from my earlier work: all of creation. I like to personally greet every saint-to-be and pass along a few words of wisdom as you start your journey.

First, the name is God with a capital "G." If you spell it "god," I might accidentally spell your destination as "hell," got it? Second, heaven has received many talented applicants for sainthood over the course of forever, so it may take a while to process your application.

On the plus side, there's no concept of time in heaven, so you probably won't notice the delay.

As you begin your journey to join heaven's elite team, keep in mind that I am the alpha and the omega. I see all, and to fall from my favor risks eternal damnation. But also, have fun with it! Very few people ultimately earn the title of "Saint," and it can be a stressful process, so remember: keep calm and carry on. Yes, I know that's a Winston Churchill quote, but as the inventor of humanity, all famous quotes are technically mine. Bazinga.

Best of luck, and we look forward to seeing you in heaven. We have a piping hot Seven Loko waiting for you! (Yes, it's hot. This shit's *insane*.)

—God

HOLY FAQ!

What is a saint?
A saint is a person who has died and gone to heaven. That's it! Everyone who has died and gone to heaven is a saint, but here's the catch: Catholics only give the title of capital "S" Saint to people they can absolutely prove are in heaven. How do you prove someone is in heaven? Through the process of canonization, which you are about to begin!

Do I have to be Catholic to be a saint?
Technically, yes. But "saint" is a pretty broad term. Lots of religions have their own versions of saints, meaning people who, due to their exemplary lives, are worthy of emulation and adoration. This book deals specifically with Catholic saints because (a) the history of the canonization process is uniquely bizarre and (b) a book that covers all saint-making processes across all religions would be too heavy to comfortably read lying down in bed.

What's the difference between a Christian and a Catholic?
Christians are people who believe in Jesus and follow the teachings of the Bible. Catholics are Christians who worship specifically in the Roman Catholic Church (meaning priests, bishops, popes, the mass—that whole deal). Christianity is a large umbrella that also covers denominations like Protestant and Orthodox Christian. Basically, all Catholics are Christians, but not all Christians are Catholics. It's like how all squares are rhombuses but not all rhombuses are squares. Now you've learned *two* things!

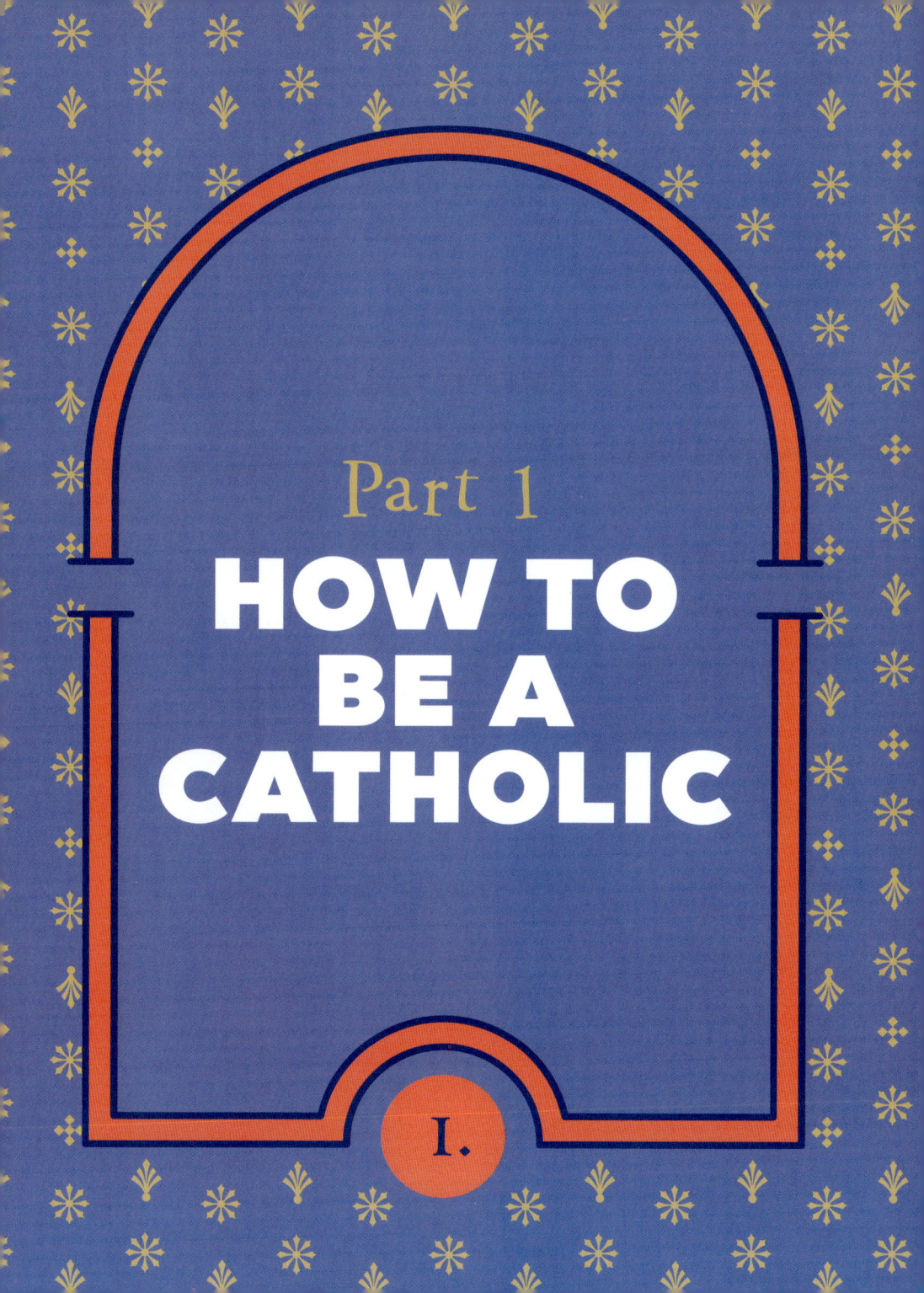

efore you kick off your journey to sainthood, there is one small detail you need to take care of: in order to become a Catholic saint, first you have to be a Catholic. It's a minor, annoying technicality, like how you have to show ID before you can buy Sudafed. Catholicism is a two-thousand-year-old religion with over a billion members worldwide and a rich history that has influenced everything from art to politics to the calendar. So, the next couple of pages should pretty much cover it.

CATHOLIC STATS

- **MEMBERSHIP:** 1.3 billion
- **LEADER:** The Pope
- **REAL LEADER:** God
- **GUY YOU LOVE TO HATE:** Satan
- **BOOK:** The Bible (anything by Dan Brown is a close second)
- **FAVORITE CHANT:** Gregorian
- **FAVORITE POSITION:** Missionary
- **HEADQUARTERS:** Vatican City

- **FLAG:** Yellow and white with the keys to heaven and a fun pope hat
- **BIGGEST STRENGTH:** Money, power, influence
- **BIGGEST WEAKNESS:** Money, power, influence

B.Y.O.B.
(Bring Your Own Baptism)

The first step in becoming Catholic is getting baptized. It's how you officially join Team Catholic. It's the draft, the varsity jacket, the whatever they do in hockey. You can be the best person in the history of the world, but if you weren't baptized, Catholic leaders won't let you be canonized as a saint. They're jerks that way.

> ### SACRAMENTS
> Sacraments are rituals performed to bring the recipient closer to the grace of God. They are broken into the sacraments of initiation (baptism, communion, confirmation), healing (penance, anointing of the sick), service (holy orders), and "it'll break your grandma's heart if you don't get married in a church" (matrimony).

Baptism is one of the seven sacraments. The others are confirmation, first communion, penance (a.k.a. confession), anointing of the sick, holy orders, and matrimony. The reason baptism is such a biggie is because it's the sacrament that washes away original sin, which Catholics believe all humans are born with because Adam and Eve screwed things up for the rest of us. Jesus received this sacrament from the aptly named John the Baptist. Hiring people must've been a lot easier back when folks were literally named for their professions.

The person receiving the sacrament, who we will call the *baptee*,[*] is blessed with either a little or a lot of water, depending on how splashy the priest is feeling that day. A baptismal candle is lit off the Paschal candle[†] to symbolize that the enlightenment of Christ has been passed on through baptism. This candle then lives in a box in your parents' attic for eternity because it feels wrong to use it like a regular candle but also feels wrong to throw it away. It eventually migrates to your own attic until someday it becomes your child's problem.[‡]

Originally, baptism was performed in adulthood, when a person could freely choose to accept the Catholic faith. Nowadays, it's typically done when the baptee[§] is an infant in order to start protecting their soul from an early age. Also, because babies in cute lil' dresses and suits are adorable.

---

[*] Not a real term. No one says this.
[†] A big candle lit every Easter to symbolize the light of Christ and increase a church's fire insurance policy.
[‡] Passing your unresolved baggage onto your children is a sacred Catholic tradition.
[§] Which again, is not a thing.

> **WHY IS IT THE ROMAN CATHOLIC CHURCH?**
> The short answer is because it follows the pope, who is also the bishop of Rome. The long answer is to distinguish it from other Catholic rites that observe slightly different traditions, but this box is small, so let's stick with the short answer.

The rite of baptism is usually performed in church with the infant's parents and godparents, but church law allows for anyone to perform baptism in cases of emergency when a priest can't be present.[¶] So, if you want to be a saint and you're in a pinch, here's all you need to have a DIY baptism:

- **WATER:** The water of baptism symbolizes washing away original sin and mimics Jesus's baptism by John the Baptist in the River Jordan. In a Catholic Church, the water is held in a baptismal font, which is usually ornate and made of marble. If you don't have an elaborate font at home, you could use a nice pot or your fanciest, least spaghetti sauce–stained Tupperware. And be sure to use a Brita to filter out the Devil.

- **OIL:** In addition to being blessed with water, the priest (or in this DIY case, whoever) anoints the person receiving baptism with a sacred oil. In a pinch, try using a nice olive oil. Not the

---

[¶] Emergency baptisms are usually performed for people with critical medical conditions, but that's not the only reason. Surely "I was too lazy and/or impatient so I just did it myself" is also acceptable!

kind you fry with, but the fancy kind that you dip bread into for an appetizer. Then after the baptism, you can use the rest for a classy snack.

- **CANDLE:** Everyone who is baptized leaves with a baptismal candle, which symbolizes that they now carry the light of Christ. For a DIY substitute, use a scented candle with a sacred-sounding name like Moonlit Walk or Pumpkin Banana Scone.

- **GODPARENTS:** Your godparents are people who accept the responsibility of praying for you and guiding you through your spiritual life. They should be faithful Catholics who are either close to or a part of your family. In reality, they are usually an odd assortment of old roommates and second cousins who were willing to put on clean clothes and show up to church on a Saturday. Can't find anybody to fill the role? Substitute your father's complete DVD set of *Godfather* movies. Your dad doesn't have one? Ask another dad. At least one in five dads has one.

- **WHITE CLOTHES:** Everyone who is baptized is supposed to wear white to symbolize purity. If you don't have the extra time or cash to run out and grab a new outfit, just use what you have on hand, like toilet paper. Wrap yourself up in Christlike white two-ply and be welcomed into the Catholic family dressed like a weird holy mummy. Plus, you'll be extra absorbent during the anointing. No cleanup!

THE BASICS

nce you're baptized, you're a Catholic. Welcome! Pull up a pew and plop a holy squat. Now it's time to live as a Catholic. Don't worry, it's pretty simple. If over a billion people can do it, you can, too. Here are the basics:

1. Go to church. Or at least plan to go to church. On Saturday night, set your alarm so you have time to shower and eat a nice breakfast before you go. Then hit snooze a few times on Sunday morning, which is fine, because you can always eat a granola bar in the car. No big deal if you hit snooze a few more times, because who cares if you're showered for church, right? Jesus didn't shower every day. When the alarm goes off a third time, transition to the couch, fall back asleep, and promise yourself you'll definitely go to church on Christmas and Easter. Or at least plan to.
2. Hang a crucifix somewhere in your house. Usually either in the kitchen or over the bed so that you forget it's there

until you catch it out of the corner of your eye during sex and feel really weird about it for the rest of the week.
3. Feel a little guilty about something all the time. What the thing is doesn't matter. Just feel bad about it.
4. Follow the teachings laid out in the *Catechism of the Catholic Church*. This is the book explaining the rules and beliefs of the Catholic religion, which the vast majority of Catholics have never actually completely read.
5. Put out a manger scene with your Christmas decorations. If you lose the baby Jesus (which is inevitable—he's the teeniest piece), replace him with something respectful like a LEGO person or a particularly cute baby carrot.
6. Have either a holy card, rosary, or Bible in a drawer somewhere that you never use but also never throw away in case you commit a really big sin someday and need it.
7. Know the chorus to at least one song by Creed. At the very least, be prepared to belt the lyric, "With arms wide open!"
8. Buy two sets of stamps for Christmas: one that is Santa Claus/snowman/holy-jolly themed and one that is baby Jesus themed for sending cards to relatives who make a whole stink about "putting the 'Christ' back in Christmas."
9. Pretend to know the difference between the Ascension and the Assumption.*
10. Every year, usually in March, say, "Oh shit, it's Lent?" and

---

* The Ascension is when Jesus went back up to heaven forty days after he rose from the dead. The Assumption is when his mother, Mary, died and went to heaven, body and soul. Or is it the other way around? Oh crap.

then remember that you forgot to give up something for Lent.
11. Follow the Ten Commandments. And don't take the Lord's name in vain, goddammit.
12. Have at least one relative who is disappointed in you.
13. Aspire to be a good person. Or, if that's too hard, shift the focus to how other people are definitely worse sinners than you.
14. Attend at least one fish fry because, on the eighth day, God created panko-encrusted tilapia.
15. Attend weddings that take forever and have a slightly too long gap between the ceremony and the reception. You will be responsible for explaining what's going on during the ceremony to your non-Catholic friends. If you don't know, just make something up. Here's a freebie: "We kneel to honor that time Jesus tore his ACL during preseason."

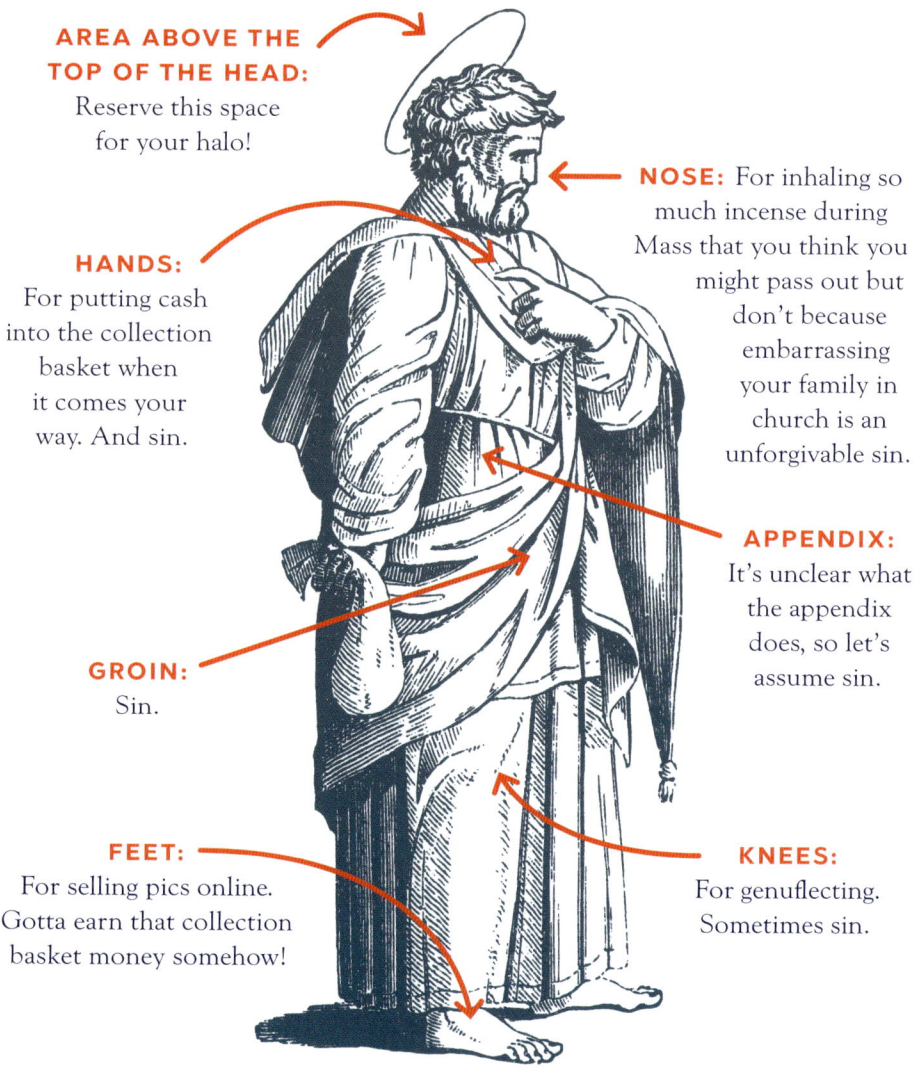

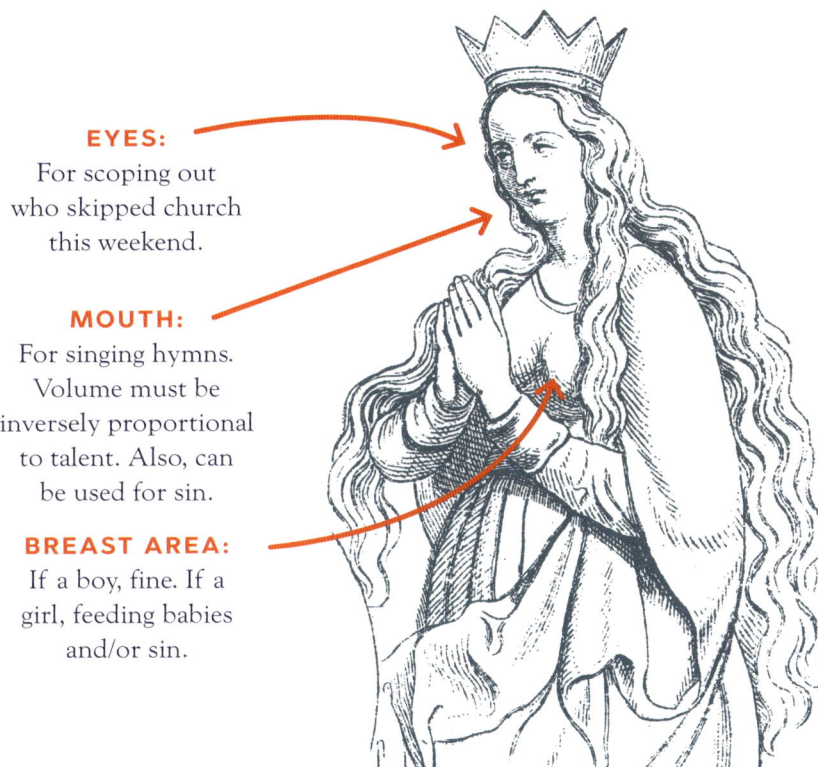

EYES: For scoping out who skipped church this weekend.

MOUTH: For singing hymns. Volume must be inversely proportional to talent. Also, can be used for sin.

BREAST AREA: If a boy, fine. If a girl, feeding babies and/or sin.

Accessories

- **Rosary:** For praying to Mary, Mother of God, and/or fidgeting with while bored during mass.
- **Scapular:** Worn to indicate a particular devotion to religious life, and because you enjoy explaining to people what a scapular is.
- **Holy card:** For praying to other saints. Collect 'em all!
- **Cash:** For elaborately placing in the offering basket so your neighbors can see how generous you are.

A POPE, BY ANY OTHER NAME

he pope has a lot of nicknames. To avoid confusion, here are a few you might come across on your journey to halo-town.

ANTIPOPE

An antipope is a person who claims to be pope but isn't. Due to intense power struggles, there have been several antipopes throughout Catholic history, many of whom ruled successfully for years. Remember, for most of human history, if a group of bishops in your region said, "Hey, this guy is pope," you didn't have the option to Google "Is that guy really pope?" You just said, "Okay, great. Hi, new pope!" There are still present-day antipopes but, unlike in the past, you can Google them.

- Pope
- Papa
- Pontiff
- Supreme Pontiff
- Holy See
- Holy Father
- His Holiness
- Bishop of Rome
- Vicar of Jesus Christ
- Successor of the Prince of the Apostles
- Supreme Pontiff of the Universal Church
- Patriarch of the West
- Primate of Italy
- Metropolitan Archbishop of the Province of Rome
- Sovereign of the State of Vatican City
- Servant of the Servants of God
- Mr. Big Shot (never to his face, though)

THE BIBLE REAL QUICK

Now that you're officially Catholic, you follow the teachings of the Bible. The Bible is a collection of seventy-three books that were written over the course of roughly two thousand years, by a ton of different people, most of whom probably didn't know Jesus personally. It's split into the Old Testament and New Testament, and each book is told in chapters and verses. Also, the print is usually pretty small and hard to read, unless it's a kid's Bible, in which case there are pictures!

It's also important to point out that not every Bible is the same. Different groups use different versions, some with different amounts of books, and in different orders. Even within Catholicism, there are different translations available. Remember, the Bible is a book, compiled of other books that have been translated, retranslated, and retranslated again and again, often from languages that aren't spoken anymore. Imagine playing a game of telephone for two thousand years, except the sentence you're passing along is the foundation for multiple religions.

No matter what version of the Bible you go with, it's a hefty book. If you've never read it and don't have the patience to listen to an audiobook, no worries. Here's a completely accurate, slightly abridged version of the whole thing:

THE OLD TESTAMENT
Pre-Jesus

- **Genesis**

    God creates everything. It ends badly.

- **Exodus**

    Moses leads the Israelites out of Egypt and receives the Ten Commandments from God. He gets mad and breaks them, which is honestly kinda rude.

- **Leviticus**

    Lots of rules about everything, including sex. For example: if you have intercourse with an animal, both you and the animal should be slain, which seems pretty harsh toward the poor animal, who was only trying to make her ex jealous.

- **Numbers**

    Hilariously contains mostly letters.

- **Deuteronomy**

    More rules. Ends with (spoiler alert!) Moses dying at the spry young age of 120.

- **Joshua**
  Joshua takes over for Moses and leads the Israelites into the Promised Land. It ends with him dying at the end at the age of 110. Impressive, but no Moses.
- **Judges**
  The Israelites have some ups and downs and judges.
- **Ruth**
  Ruth marries Boas and has a son. She also has a fantastic, healthy relationship with her mother-in-law, so of course historians believe this story is fictional.
- **The First Book of Samuel**
  Really just a prequel to the Second Book of Samuel when David becomes king of Israel.
- **The Second Book of Samuel**
  David becomes king of Israel!
- **The First Book of Kings**
  A chronicle of the kings of Israel. This is where you'll find that famous parable about King Solomon cutting the baby in half.*
- **The Second Book of Kings**
  More kings. No Solomon.
- **The First Book of Chronicles, The Second Book of Chronicles, Ezra, Nehemiah**
  These four books chronicle the history of the kingdom of Judah. They are considered four parts that go together, like how they split up *The Hobbit* into three movies.

---

* He didn't actually do it. No babies were harmed in the making of this parable.

- **Tobit**

    Tobit met an archangel. Neat!

- **Judith**

    Recounts the story of Judith, a young Jewish woman, and Holofernes, the commander of an Assyrian army. Holofernes leads his troops against the Jewish population so, to save them, Judith seduces Holofernes, waits until he's drunk and asleep, and cuts his head off. The story is likely fictional, but the famous painting inspired by it is cool as hell.

"Good morning! Have a KNIFE day! Ugh, never mind, that sounded so much cooler in my head." —Judith

❧ **Esther**
Esther becomes queen and sadly doesn't get to behead anybody.

❧ **The First Book of Maccabees**
Political and military history of Judea.

❧ **The Second Book of Maccabees**
Attack of the Clones

❧ **Job**
Lotsa bad shit happens to Job.

❧ **Psalms**
A collection of early hymns. We don't know the tune, so feel free to make one up! "Row, Row, Row Your Boat" works surprisingly well.

❧ **Proverbs**
Short, poetic nuggets of wisdom. Like a Biblical version of a "hang in there" cat poster.

❧ **Ecclesiastes**
You know that expression, "There's nothing new under the sun"? That's from this! Also, if you didn't know that expression, now you do! Thanks, Ecclesiastes!

❧ **The Song of Songs**
People magazine's Sexiest Book of the Bible. Begins with, "Let him kiss me with kisses of his mouth!" NSFW.

❧ **Wisdom**
Contains wisdom and trace amounts of peanuts.

❧ **Sirach**
Long, extremely detailed book about how to be a good person,

including, "do not chew greedily." So, if you're chewing bubble gum right now, spit it out, sinner.

- **Isaiah**

    Isaiah is a prophet who tells of a coming messiah, who Catholics believe is Jesus. Could also be titled, "There's a Messiah at the End of This Book."

- **Jeremiah**

    Was a bullfrog.

- **Lamentations**

    Pretty fun! Just kidding. Lots of lamenting.

- **Baruch, Ezekiel, Daniel, Hosea, Joel, Amos, Obadiah, Jonah, Micah, Nahum, Habakkuk, Zephaniah, Haggai, Zechariah, Malachi**

    Look, there are a lot of books in the Old Testament. Can most Catholics tell you what's in the Book of Nahum? Hell no. Get the bullet points and keep your head down if you run into any Bible authors in heaven. Just say generic things like, "Wow, love your work! What's my favorite? How do I even pick? It's all so good!"

THE NEW TESTAMENT
Stop. It's Jesus time.

> ### GOSPELS
> When Catholics refer to the Gospels, they are talking about the four chapters in the Bible that describe the life and resurrection of Jesus: Matthew, Mark, Luke, and John. They all tell slightly different versions of the same story. It's like how, after a night out partying with friends, you all get together the next morning to piece together the events of the previous night. Except in the case of the Gospels, the story always ends with one of the friends being crucified and resurrected, which, ideally, is not how you party.

- **The Gospel According to Matthew**
  An account of Jesus's life from birth to death. Probably not written by Matthew.
- **The Gospel According to Mark**
  Tells the story of Jesus's life from baptism to death. Was probably the first Gospel written, but probably not by Mark.
- **The Gospel According to Luke**
  An account of Jesus's life from birth to death to resurrection. If you love this, the same author wrote The Acts of the Apostles.
- **The Gospel According to John**
  Less a historical retelling of Jesus's life and more an artistic

"best of." Recounts some of Jesus's miracles and how he gathered the apostles. Probably—you guessed it—not written by John.

> ### SYNOPTIC GOSPELS
> Matthew, Mark, and Luke are known as the synoptic gospels because they are so similar, even down to some identical phrases. Let this be a lesson: if you're going to copy each other's homework, be sure to change up the wording a little so God doesn't catch you!

- **The Acts of the Apostles**
  Talks about what the Apostles did after Jesus was killed and then rose and then left again.
- **The Letter to the Romans**
  Summary: "Hi, glad to be here. Wanted to clear up some stuff about how to be a good Christian. Okay, off to Jerusalem. Smell ya later, Paul."
- **The First Letter to the Corinthians, The Second Letter to the Corinthians, The Letter to the Galatians, The Letter to the Ephesians, The Letter to the Philippians, The Letter to the Colossians**
  Also written by Paul. He wrote a lot of letters.
- **The Thank-You Note to Your Grandmother**
  Not a book of the Bible, just a nice thing to do!

- **The First Letter to the Thessalonians**
  Another letter written by our main man Paul.
- **The Second Letter to the Thessalonians**
  Could've been an email.
- **The First Letter to Timothy, The Second Letter to Timothy, The Letter to Titus, The Letter to Philemon**
  Okay, so Paul wrote a ton of letters, including all of these. He basically traveled the world evangelizing and helping establish what the post-Jesus church would look like. His letters are incredibly detailed and long and constitute the bulk of the New Testament. He would've been a very annoying pen pal.
- **The Letter to the Hebrews**
  A more general letter that doesn't include the traditional salutation or conclusion. For that reason, nobody is sure who wrote it, so most folks assume it's Paul.
- **The Letter of James**
  Sort of an open letter concerning things like perseverance, faith, patience, and the importance of prayer. Short and sweet.
- **The First Letter of Peter, The Second Letter of Peter**
  Peter's hot takes on suffering, persecution, and the Second Coming of Christ, that were maybe but also maybe not actually written by Peter.
- **The First Letter of John**
  J.
- **The Second Letter of John**
  O.

- **The Third Letter of John**
  H.
- **The Letter of Jude**
  Mostly warning people to avoid heresy. Super short. Compared to ole windbag Paul, this is basically a tweet.
- **The Book of Revelation**
  Apocalypse shit.

> **HOW TO BE A CATHOLIC CHECKLIST:**
> ✓ Get baptized.
> ✓ Be Catholic.
> ✓ Read the Bible (optional).

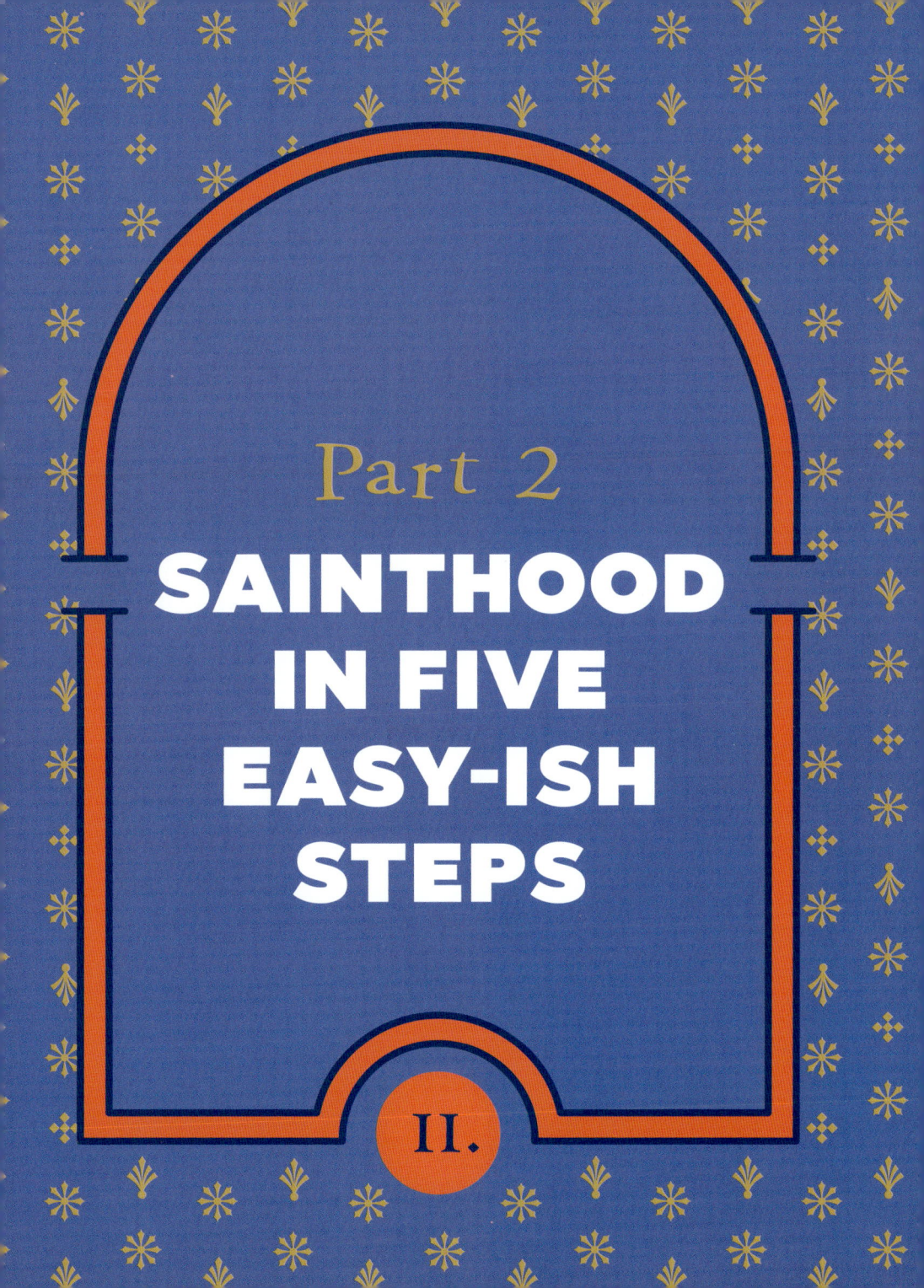

QUIZ: WHAT KIND OF SAINT ARE YOU?

Saints come in all shapes, sizes, and flavors. Use the following quiz to help narrow down what type of holy hero you want to be.

Are you a nun, priest, monk, pope, etc.?
A. Yes.
B. No.
C. I tried but couldn't sell enough cookies.
D. Wait, I'm thinking of Girl Scouts.

If you are a nun, priest, monk, pope, etc., why did you join?
A. I felt called by God.
B. I hate picking out a different outfit every day.
C. I lost a bet.
D. To avoid a shitty marriage.

Are you real?
A. Yes.
B. No.

C. Sort of.
D. We all live in a computer simulation.

Are you a loner? Also, how do you feel about deserts?
A. Yes. I need a few decades alone in the desert to recharge.
B. Sometimes. I only need like a year or two alone in the desert to recharge.
C. Kind of. I keep a small group of friends and we live near a desert.
D. No, and I hate deserts. Too harsh on the skin.

How many people have you killed?
A. Lost count.
B. None. Also, what?
C. Everyone gets one mulligan.
D. Technically, none. But the army I led? Tons.

Are any of your immediate relatives also saints?
A. They certainly think so.
B. Hard no.
C. Yes, but I'm really a self-made saint.
D. Those losers are beatified at best.

After you died, what happened to your body?
A. It decomposed.
B. It decomposed but way slower than you'd expect.
C. Um. I'm alive and reading a book?
D. It didn't decompose at all and smelled great!

Have you ever had sex?

A. Yes.
B. No.
C. Wow, that's pretty personal.
D. Just hand stuff.

Can you fly?

A. Only first class.
B. Yes.
C. No.
D. I jumped off the garage once as a kid and broke both of my arms.

If you were a food, what would you be?

A. Something sweet.
B. Something savory.
C. Something bitter.
D. A hotdog.

Are you an animal?

A. Bark.
B. Meow.
C. No.
D. Neigh.

ANSWER KEY

Mostly As: You're a super holy hermit with a bad-boy side.

Mostly Bs: You're fictional, so technically you can be whomever you want!

Mostly Cs: You're a mysterious loner.

Mostly Ds: You're incorruptible and proud of it.

Mostly Es: You took the wrong test.

AN INTRODUCTION FROM ME, SAINT ULRICH OF AUGSBURG, THE FIRST CATHOLIC SAINT

Hey, it's me. Saint Ulrich. As the first official saint of the Catholic Church, it's my privilege to welcome you on your journey to sainthood. Ah, the wonders of being a saint! The excitement of having a tiny statue of you in the back of a church somewhere. The honor of being on a holy card that sits in a drawer forever because nobody knows if it's a sin to throw it away. The sexiness of being Mr. July in the free church calendar hanging in your nana's kitchen. Wow. What a cool gig.

Just in case sarcasm has changed since I died in 973, let me be clear: I'm joking. Being a saint blows.

Why do I think that? Oh gee, maybe because I was the FIRST FREAKING SAINT and you've probably never heard of me! Sure, there were *technically* saints before me, but there was no vetting process. I was the first person to be officially investigated and approved by a pope. The Church flirted with a lot of dead guys in the early days, but I was the first saint they went steady with.

While we're at it, why am I Saint Ulrich *of Augsburg*? What, were we drowning in Ulrichs? Name *one* other than Skeet. Go ahead. I'll wait. I literally have eternity.

An Introduction from Me, Saint Ulrich of Augsburg, the First Catholic Saint ✳ 35

And where are all the kids named after me? Where's the parade for Saint Ulrich's Day? You know what I'm the patron saint of? Not fainting. As if people who are about to faint have a second to stop and think, "Oops! Better pray to Saint Ulrich real quick!" But that's not all. It's also said that touching my pastoral cross can heal people who've been bitten by rabid dogs. That one doesn't come up a whole lot now that hospitals and fences have caught on.

Sainthood is a popularity contest. Everyone who gets to heaven is all, "Wow! Can I meet Joan of Arc?" I get it. She led the French army and was burned at the stake. *Sooo cool.* But who the hell wants to spend eternity hanging out with a nineteen-year-old who smells like charred hair? Nineteen-year-olds are already the *worst* people. Now imagine one who literally believed she was chosen by God and was RIGHT. Meanwhile, I lived to be eighty-three years old! Do you know how impressive that is for the tenth century?! It's like finding out your neighbor's dog is twenty!

I lived my whole life as a model of morality, and now the only thing people know about me—if anything—is this painting of me holding a fish like a dick.

So, if you want to be a saint, go for it. Just don't come crying to me when they paint you holding a cantaloupe like a vagina or something.

"Maybe we could try some other poses?" —Ulrich

STEP 1
Die

ongrats on starting your journey to sainthood! Let's get the bad news out of the way: the first rule of sainthood is that you have to be dead. Since you are reading this book, odds are you're currently alive. Bummer. But, on the bright side, life is just a slow, lonely crawl into the cold arms of inescapable death, so you're off to a great start!

Now for the good news: the second rule of sainthood is that all the rules for becoming a saint are subject to change. The criteria for earning a halo have shifted radically throughout history, so if you don't tick all the boxes just yet, don't worry. Rules were made to be broken (except for that first one—you definitely have to be dead).

According to current church law, anyone who wants to be considered for sainthood has to be dead for at least five years... unless they are famously holy like Mother Theresa or Pope John Paul II. Again, remember the second rule: all the rules are subject to change.

The five-year rule was put into place in 1983 by Pope John Paul II. Prior to that, you had to be dead for fifty years before the canonization process could begin. The goal of this rule was to ensure that the saint-to-be's holiness wasn't a passing fad. The now obvious downside of waiting fifty years to investigate someone's life is that there's probably not much evidence of their life left. Remember, for most of history, forty was geriatric. It's pretty hard to figure out if a person's life was virtuous when all of the eyewitnesses died a generation ago.

Even with the newly shortened five-year rule, canonization still takes a long-ass time. One of the quickest canonizations in recent history was Saint Thérèse de Lisieux in 1925, who was canonized twenty-eight years after her death. Pope John Paul II especially benefited from shortening the canonization timeline, since he himself was promoted to saint just nine years after he died. But they are anomalies. The average time between funeral and canonization is 181 years. Part of the reason it's so hard to make a saint is that, for most of history, it was way too easy.

"Canonization" literally means adding someone's name to a list. In this case, it refers to the list of saints whom Catholics are officially allowed to venerate. It wasn't until 1243 that Pope Gregory IX made canonization a right exclusive to the pope. Gregory IX and his successors set up a sort of spiritual justice system by which prospective saints would be put on holy trials at the Vatican in order to verify whether they were virtuous enough to be universally venerated by the Church. It was like *Law & Order* only instead of Benson and Stabler you had a bunch of guys in robes and funny hats.

Before the popes started tightening their grip, saint making was a local, organic, farm-fresh process. Communities would start worshiping somebody, that person's story would become legendary, a cult* would form around them, the local bishop would give his stamp of holy approval, and boom: saint. What this loosey-goosey process lacked in quality it more than made up for in quantity. In the early days of the Church there were *lots* of saints. It's hard to know exactly how many, because most records were kept only at the local level. One of the most detailed lists of saints available is the *Acta Sanctorum*, which is sixty-eight volumes long. At least as of right now. The men who began writing this collection in the 1600s died before they could finish, and their predecessors are still adding to it to this day. So really, the easiest way to become a saint is to build a time machine and go back to the days when any Saint Tom, Saint Dick, and Saint Harry could make it to heaven.

This open-door sainthood policy led to obvious quality control issues. In the early twelfth century, a bishop in Sweden got caught supporting sainthood for a local "martyr" who was actually killed in a drunken brawl. Cool, but not exactly Christlike. Of course, giving power to the pope didn't fix everything. In 1369, Pope Urban V canonized Saint Elzear, who may have been a great guy but conveniently was also Urban V's godfather.†

Centralizing the canonization process under the pope wasn't just about upping the quality of saints—it was also about upping the power of the papacy. The pope wasn't always the be-all and end-all of the Church. In fact, for most of early church history, "pope" was

---

* "Cult" in the "religious devotion to a person" sense, not in the "put on your matching pajamas and drink the Kool-Aid" sense.
† For a long time, getting a job in heaven was a lot like getting a job in the entertainment industry.

a pretty weak job. So weak, in fact, that from 1378 to 1417 there were between two and three separate popes all vying for power. It's called the Papal Schism, the Great Schism, the Western Schism, or the Great Western Schism, because in true Catholic fashion, no one can even agree on what to call its most famous disagreement.[†]

> **POPE**
>
> The pope is the head of the Catholic Church and is elected by the College of Cardinals whenever the previous pope dies or resigns. Whoever is pope is considered to be in direct line from Saint Peter, the apostle and first pope. The pope is also the bishop of Rome and the monarch of Vatican City. He gets a flashy hat and a fun car. It's a big job.

Each successive generation of popes has tried to clarify and refine the canonization process, taking control of what used to be a neat local tradition and shoving it into the bureaucratic black hole of fun that is the Vatican. And a lot has changed: the stages of approval, the timeline, the cost, even the shape of halos. But the one thing that has remained the same and is your unavoidable first step on the way to sainthood is: you've gotta die. But get excited, because if there's one thing the Catholic Church loves, it's a cool death.

[†] It was truly a wonderful hot mess that included all sides excommunicating each other. If reality television had existed then, this would've been bigger than *The Bachelor*.

> **STEP 1: CHECKLIST**
> ✓ Be famous (if possible, for something good).
> ✓ Die.

Post-Death Options for Catholics

Once you're dead, you've got to go somewhere. Here are what the Catholic Church has determined to be your choices:

Heaven

Heaven is where it's at. The goal. Eternal bliss. The Bible describes heaven as the "firmament" (a.k.a. sky), which led to the contemporary view that heaven is up and hell is down. It's also why many churches and cathedrals paint heaven on the ceiling. Heaven is where the dead are reunited with their loved ones, and where they find out which loved ones didn't make the cut. Heaven is also where the faithful finally see God, which results in pure happiness. You can only reach heaven if you are free from sin, which means you have to be really damn good, or spend a little time in purgatory.

Purgatory

If you aren't bad enough to go to hell but aren't quite good enough to go straight to heaven, Catholics believe you go to a place called purgatory. Purgatory is a temporary hell, much like flying out of Newark. Souls go there to work off any lingering sins from life before they proceed to heaven. Saints can intercede on behalf of souls in purgatory, so once you earn your halo, you can help out your friends and family members who were a little on the shitty side.

Hell

Hell is the opposite of heaven, meaning it is the eternal absence of God a.k.a. happiness. Hell is run by Satan, who is a fallen angel. Prior to fighting with God and getting banished from heaven, Satan only knew eternal bliss, which explains why he's so mad all the time. Historically, hell is portrayed as a place of fire and torture. Though what's usually portrayed is bodily pain, spiritual pain is the real punishment, since hell is the loss of God's comfort. And, as anyone who has ever slept multiple nights on a futon knows, loss of comfort is truly hell.

Limbo (But Not Anymore)

For a long time, Catholics were taught there was a fourth option called limbo. This was the destination for good people who had the unfortunate luck of dying before Jesus existed. More importantly, it's where babies went if they died before they could be baptized. Baptism is the sacrament that washes away original sin, so without it, Catholics—even innocent babies—weren't eligible for heaven. While limbo solved a theological loophole, it became pretty unpopular because...obviously. There's a reason you don't see many sympathy cards that read, "Sorry for your loss. You will never meet your dead baby in heaven." The Church officially dropped limbo from its teachings in 2007 because it turns out, if you think about it for even a second, the concept of limbo absolutely sucks.

Is Martyrdom Right for Me?

So, you want to make it to heaven, but you're not sure how to get there? One tried-and-true route is martyrdom. Fair warning: it can get a little messy.

A martyr is anyone (not just a Catholic) who dies for their faith. In the earliest days of the Church, martyrdom was the main way to become a saint. Each church had its own "martyrology": a list of local martyrs who could be venerated and prayed to for intercession. The logic was that, by suffering and dying like Christ, martyrs were the only people the public could be sure definitely went to heaven.

"Ugh, sorry guys! This ascent to heaven will be way easier once escalators are invented!"

> **INTERCESSION**
>
> This is what it's called when a saint acts on behalf of humans in heaven. By praying to saints, humans ask them to intervene and put in a good word with the Big Guy. Saints are heaven's middle management.

Luckily (or unluckily), martyrdom was a pretty common fate in the early days. The Roman emperors were never huge fans of Christians, but things really took a turn in 64 CE* when a fire nearly destroyed the city. Emperor Nero needed somebody to blame for the tragedy, and Christians were a slam dunk. They were new, weird, didn't worship Roman gods, and their belief system bucked the fragile social order of the ever-expanding empire. Nero said that obviously, the fire was the Christians' fault (and not, you know, densely packed flammable buildings). Things went downhill from there, and eventually Christianity was outlawed and made punishable by death.

> **VENERATION**
>
> Basically, a religious version of showing admiration and respect. Catholic saints are venerated, not worshiped. This means you can pray to them for help, but they don't actually do the helping. Catholics aren't allowed to worship saints—they only worship God. That's one of the Ten Commandments, which, if you haven't yet, you should probably read. There will be a pop quiz when you arrive in heaven.

---

* Okay, so CE and BCE stand for Common Era and Before the Common Era. This is the contemporary, secularized way of expressing time. You may also sometimes see AD/BC, which stand for *Anno Domini* (Latin for "in the year of our Lord") and Before Christ. This is a reference to the Gregorian calendar, which bases time on when Jesus was born. Common Era also uses the Gregorian calendar. Also, nobody knows exactly when Jesus was born, but—spoiler alert—it probably wasn't in 1 AD/CE anyways.

But these people didn't just die. They gruesomely, grossly, spectacularly died. Here is a short list of just some of the ways in which early Christian martyrs were killed:

- Burned alive
- Teeth ripped out, then burned alive
- Head chopped off
- Shot with arrows
- Stoned
- Clubbed
- Stabbed
- Roasted
- Pressed
- Dismembered
- Beat to death with school supplies[*]
- Crucified
- Upside-down crucified
- Fed to wild animals
- Tied to a breaking wheel (which does what it says)
- Thrown down a well
- Tied to two palm trees that are bent to the ground and secured with rope, then the rope gets cut so the trees snap back into place and rip your body in half[†]
- Flayed
- Anchor tied to neck and thrown into the sea
- Any combination of the above
- And more!

A little extreme? Absolutely. But in the defense of these ancient killers, the internet hadn't been invented yet, so there wasn't a ton to do.

---

[*] By his own students!
[†] This was the extremely creative and super-gross martyrdom of Saint Corona.

The heyday for martyrdom was prior to the fourth century. Between 250 and 311 CE the Roman Empire sentenced tens of thousands of Christians to death. Surprisingly, the prospect of a gruesome death wasn't that big of a deterrent to early Christians. In fact, it seems to have done the opposite. During that same period, the number of Christians more than doubled. If anything, the volume of martyrs seems to have made this plucky new religion more famous, which just goes to show that all press is good press.

The fun ended in 313 when the first Christian emperor, Constantine, signed the Edict of Milan, which stated that Christians were allowed to believe whatever they wanted. Sounds like good news, but by then, martyrdom had become a badge of honor. Christians desired the opportunity to die like Christ. Remember that "teeth ripped out, then burned alive" from the earlier list? That's Saint Apollonia (d. 249), who got a free total extraction from an angry mob who were demanding that she renounce her religion. They threatened to burn her alive, so she beat them to the punch by *voluntarily* jumping onto a burning pyre. That's one way to deal with dental pain.

The end of the martyr boom caused an odd problem for a religion that prized paradise in death. Remember, up until this point, saints were almost exclusively martyrs. To keep up with the times, the Church had to start reevaluating what made a person saint material. Over time, the focus of sainthood shifted from confirming a person's virtuous death to investigating whether they led a virtuous life. Though less common now than it used to

Saint Apollonia who is, unfortunately, the patron saint of dentists.

be, martyrdom does still exist and comes with its own canonization perks. To become a saint, a candidate needs to perform at least two miracles, but according to canon law, anyone who is martyred gets a pass on one of the two miracle requirements. So, if you're looking for a 50-percent-off-canonization coupon, martyrdom may be the way to go.

> **CANON LAW**
>
> Canon law is the Church's legal system. It covers everything from the rules of canonization, to how popes are elected, to how to get an annulment. Many colleges offer programs where you can get a JCL (*Juris Canonici Licentiatus*)—basically a law degree for Catholicism. It's helpful to have someone with a JCL on your team when you are attempting canonization, so go butter up some Catholic law students. They're like regular law students, but their crippling debt comes with bonus crippling guilt.

Tips for the Aspiring Martyr

Becoming a martyr has historically been a surefire way to fast-track your trip to heaven. But what options are left in this post–feed-Christians-to-lions world? It's a good question. It's also why, starting in the twentieth century, popes have been slowly expanding the definition of martyrdom to include a new category called "martyr of charity." A martyr of charity is someone who dies while protecting either another person or the truth. If that sounds vague—great! That means more potential routes to heaven for you!

Martyrdom sounds scary (because it is), but it makes the path to sainthood much easier. Martyrs get to skip one of the miracle requirements in the canonization process and tend to be venerated by the public quickly because their deaths grab a lot of attention. Just try to be martyred solo. Large groups of martyrs are often canonized together, like the Martyrs of Japan (1597), the Martyrs of Mexico (twentieth century), and the Martyrs of Paraguay (1628). These folks are all in heaven, but we here on Earth usually know of them only as a collective. You want to be Gladys Knight, not the Pips.

If you want to give martyrdom a try but are a little nervous about the whole "horrific death" part, here are a few fun, new, and (relatively) pain-free death options for the aspiring martyr:

- Slip and fall while entering church, preferably on your way to an early mass so people are amazed at your willingness to wake up early on a weekend.
- Slather yourself in peanut butter and jump into a pen of puppies. For this to count as dying for your faith, you'll have to do it while trying to convert the puppies to Christianity. Technically, this one only works if you're allergic to both peanut butter and puppies. Otherwise, it's just a delightful afternoon.
- Push a convincing dummy out of an airplane then dive out to try to "save" it. To drive the point home, you'll have to shout, "I'll save you! Also, I'm Catholic and my name is [your name here], and I would make a great saint!" right before you jump.

As long as the other people in the plane don't notice that the dummy is fake, don't see that you actually pushed it out, and don't ask a ton of follow-up questions about what the hell just happened, you could qualify to be a martyr of charity!

- Attempt to evangelize Mars. If Martians exist and decide to kill you for being Catholic, you get to be a saint *and* the person who discovered Martians! That's the rare secular/religious combo win!
- Say the Virgin Mary came to you in a vision and told you to eat nothing but donuts for the rest of your life. This will eventually kill you. Sadly, to make it count as "Christlike suffering," you'll have to make them old-fashioned donuts.
- Get ripped apart by *three* palm trees. This alone may not qualify you as a martyr, but at least it means you went on a fun, tropical vacation before dying.

> **RED VS. WHITE MARTYRS**
>
> There are typically two types of martyrs. Red martyrs are people who die bloody, gruesome deaths (hence the red). Think Joan of Arc being burned at the stake, Peter being crucified upside-down, Stephen being stoned to death—you get the idea. On the flip side are white martyrs who die a symbolic death to the world by living lives of isolation and deprivation. Think hermits. This also includes people who were persecuted for their faith but never actually shed blood. White and red martyrs are also sometimes referred to as dry and wet martyrs, which also makes sense but sounds way more gross.

Saints Who Probably Joined Religious Orders Just to Avoid Shitty Marriages

At this point you might be asking yourself, "Am I pursuing sainthood for the right reasons?" The answer is probably no, but don't worry about it! Lots of saints took nontraditional paths toward the pearly gates. Especially these ladies.

Unless you've been living in isolation, never watched TV or movies, and never read a book, you may have noticed that historically, women have gotten the shit end of the stick. This was especially true in ancient times, when marriage was a transaction between families and not as God intended: the result of a game show where you date between twenty and thirty men at the same time and slowly eliminate them via rose ceremony.

To avoid getting married off to men three times their age and popping out kids until it literally killed them, a lot of women turned to religious orders where they could be granted some level of power over their bodies and could maybe even learn to do wild stuff like read and write. Given the available options, it's hard to view it as a coincidence that the following saints just happened to hear Christ calling them when wedding bells started to ring.

Saint Catherine of Siena (d. 1380)

Catherine was one of twenty-five children (so arguably, her mother was the saint). When Catherine was sixteen, her sister died, leaving behind a horny widower. The family offered up Catherine as a replacement wife, but wouldn't ya know it, at that exact moment Catherine realized she couldn't get married because she was devoted to Christ. She must've been very disappointed not to be sold off to her brother-in-law like a spare part. She lived her life in religious devotion and ended up dying at the age of thirty-three of a stroke induced by extreme fasting—but not before founding a monastery for women, actively working for peace in Italy, and

"Is the crown of thorns too much? I feel like maybe it's too much." —Catherine

learning how to read and write. She also had stigmata that only she could see. Convenient.

Saint Agatha of Sicily (d. circa 251)

Beating Catherine, Agatha was only fifteen when a Roman official came courting, demanding her hand in marriage. Being a devout Catholic from a well-off family, Agatha wasn't in the mood to settle and instead declared a life of religious chastity. The Roman man respected Agatha's wishes and moved on. Just kidding. He had her

"Who ordered the 34Bs?" —Agatha

"You've got to be kidding me." —Agatha

thrown into a brothel, then a prison, where she was tortured and had her breasts chopped off. Agatha eventually died in prison, all while refusing the marriage that would have guaranteed her freedom. Agatha's devotion to Christ in the face of unimaginable torture has made her a well-known and respected saint in Italy, where she is unfortunately commemorated with cakes shaped like her lopped-off tits.

Saint Rita of Cascia (d. 1457)

Unlike Agatha and Catherine, Rita was unsuccessful at avoiding marriage. Despite begging her parents to allow her to join a convent, Rita was married off at the ripe old age of twelve. She had two sons and a pretty miserable home life until her husband was killed in a fight when she was thirty. Here's where poor Rita's story takes a sharp turn. Her teenage sons went out to avenge their father's death. Not wanting them to end up murderers, Rita allegedly prayed that God would strike her sons down dead before they could do the deed. Seems like she could've started with something a little less extreme, like praying that God change their minds, or for their horse to break down or something. Unfortunately for her sons, Rita's prayers worked. The boys contracted a fatal illness and died before finding their father's killer. Rita lived out the rest of her life in a convent and ironically is a patron saint of parenthood. So, kids, the next time your mother says she's praying to Saint Rita—look out.

Saint Etheldreda (d. 679)

Etheldreda was one of four daughters named, and I shit you not, Ethelburga, Withburga, and Sexburga. All the sisters were royalty who became nuns and eventually became saints. When she was a teenager, Etheldreda's plan to become a nun was interrupted by her father, King Anna of East Anglia, who married her off to a prince named Tonbert. Luckily, the prince died before the marriage could be consummated, so Etheldreda went back to Plan A and continued her religious studies. Unfortunately, King Dad married her off *again*, this time to a prince named Egfrid. This time, Etheldreda proposed a compromise: they could get married but would live like brother and sister so she could maintain her vow of chastity. For pretty obvious reasons, Egfrid* was not a fan of this plan. They took the case to the local bishop who, sadly for Egfrid, sided with Etheldreda. She lived out the rest of her life as a blissfully chaste nun like her sisters who, again—and I'm not kidding—were named Ethelburga, Withburga, and Sexburga.

Saint Alexius (Early Fifth Century)

Not every saint who found God to get out of marriage was a woman. Saint Alexius was a young man from a well-off family who felt called to religious life. His parents disagreed, and they forced young Alexius to marry against his will. Determined not to be a husband, Alexius turned to his new bride for mercy, telling her he'd had a vision calling him to a life of service. Not exactly what a bride wants to hear on her wedding day, but she agreed to release him. Alexius didn't give her a chance to change her mind and fled town on his wedding night.

---

* Egfrid was fifteen at the time, so understandably he was pretty pumped about having sex.

Alexius lived the hermit life for years, praying, giving to the poor, and hiding his true identity. But he couldn't get over how much he missed his family, so he returned home. Sadly, his parents and wife[†] didn't recognize him. Thinking he was a common beggar, they agreed to let him stay as long as he lived under the staircase of the house. He lived there for seventeen years and was finally found dead one day, clutching a letter explaining who he truly was. Might've been more helpful to have said that when he first came home, but hey, to each hermit his own.

"You get me, staircase."
—Alexius

Saints Who Are Sort of Like Zombies

You've probably noticed by now that death and Catholicism go together like chips and guac. You can have chips without guac, but guac without chips? That makes no sense. In this analogy, Catholicism is the guac. Anyway, the main focus for most Catholics is whether their immortal soul goes up or down after death. But what happens to the body you leave behind matters a lot, too. Especially if you're a saint.

[†] Because they were technically married before he left, the wife had no choice but to live the rest of her celibate life with her in-laws, which some would argue is a bigger sacrifice than Alexius being a hermit.

> **JUDGMENT DAY**
>
> A.k.a The Last Judgment, a.k.a. The Second Coming, a.k.a. Oops The End of the World. Here's how it goes down: the dead are resurrected, Jesus comes back with all the angels and sorts out who was good and who was bad, then he takes the good folks to heaven with him. Much like in high school, judgment could happen at any time, so have fun never relaxing!

To understand why these bodies are so important, you have to understand that the resurrection of Jesus Christ is the central miracle of Catholicism. It's why the most sacred holiday for Catholics is Easter.[*] Catholics believe that, three days after his death, Jesus Christ arose body and soul and ascended to heaven. They also believe that our souls will be reunited with our bodies on Judgment Day, which might make things a little messy for folks who were cremated.

All dead bodies are special, but dead saint bodies are extra special. "Rest in peace" doesn't really apply to saints-to-be because Catholics believe God can work miracles through the physical remains of saints. That's why their bodies are exhumed and preserved as relics. It's also why, sometimes, those bodies are found to be incorrupt.

Incorruption is when the body of a saint doesn't show signs of decay or rigor mortis but remains "moist and flexible."[†] So incorrupt

---

[*] Sorry, Christmas.
[†] This is an actual quote from one of the main texts on this subject, *The Incorruptibles* by Joan Carroll Cruz. It's also the grossest and best description of the human condition ever written.

saints aren't like zombies in the sense that they eat brains, but in the sense that they exhibit unnaturally lifelike qualities long after they should definitely be totally dead. The first recorded saint to have been found incorrupt was Saint Cecilia. Cecilia was martyred around the year 177[†] for refusing to renounce her religion to Roman officials. They attempted to suffocate her to death and, when that didn't work, sent an executioner to chop off her head. Unfortunately, that executioner had a bad day at work and flubbed the job. He only partially severed her head, leaving her to die slowly over the course of three days. He then fled the scene, hopefully to go file his resignation because head-chopping really isn't something you get to be "just okay" at.

In 1599, Cecilia's body was exhumed and found with no signs of decay in exactly the same position she reportedly died in. Both her clothing and casket were also fully intact. Her body reportedly let off a sweet smell, which means at least one gross lil' freak said, "Hey, lemme sniff that body that's been dead for fourteen hundred years."

There are natural explanations for unintended preservation. Bodies can be found mummified in arid climates or frozen in cold ones. But in most cases, those bodies would still be dried out and stiff. Plus, in many cases of incorruption, the bodies are found alongside other bodies that have decayed normally. To drive home the point of heavenly intervention, many incorrupt bodies also show other miraculous signs like smelling nice, glowing with rays of light, emitting oils, or bleeding. Even if they eventually decay due to human interference

---

[†] There is some debate over when Cecilia actually lived and whether or not these events are even true, but it's a good story, so here we go!

after exhumation, the saint is still considered to be incorrupt as long as they are originally found to be—you guessed it—"moist and flexible."*

The incorruptibles are a pretty small club: just over a hundred official cases in the history of Catholicism. If you're considering joining this elite group, you'll want to start eating potpourri and snorting Botox now.† You'll also want to learn from the best.

Saint Albert the Great (c. 1206–1280)

Albert the Great is considered a Doctor of the Church, meaning he wrote a lot of stuff and is generally a big deal. Unlike a lot of his fellow saints, Albert lived a long and wonderful life and died peacefully at the age of seventy-four. Three years after his death, his body was exhumed and found to be fully intact and emitting a nice smell. It's Albert's second exhumation where things get tricky. He was moved in 1483, and this time his body was, to put it in medical

"Hang on, lemme write this down: 'Help me Obi-Wan Kenobi. You're my only hope.'" —Albert the Great

---

* So icky. Thanks, Joan!
† Sadly necessary disclaimer: don't eat potpourri or snort Botox.

terms, a mess. He was mostly bones but had intact eyes, most of his beard, one ear, and feet. But he still smelled great! He was placed in a glass coffin where he sat on display until the 1800s, despite being in a state many might describe as freaking terrifying. Today, like a normal corrupt body, all that's left of Albert is bones. No word on how the bones smell.

Saint Charbel Makhlouf (1828–1898)

Saint Charbel was a pretty normal monk. He spent a lot of time alone in prayer, practiced self-mortification, died at the age of seventy, and was buried according to the rules of his religious order: straight in the ground with no embalming and no coffin. The only reason anyone took notice of him after his death was because a bright light glowed from his tomb for forty-five nights after his burial. After what one has to imagine were forty-five pretty freaked-out nights, his fellow monks received permission to exhume his body. Not only was Charbel found to be incorrupt but, after a series of rainstorms, his body was actually found floating in mud, which is traditionally not a great way to preserve a body. Charbel was cleaned, clothed, and placed in a nice coffin when an additional, even freakier thing occurred: a mix of blood and sweat began to flow out of his pores. Now, a normal person might see that and run away so fast they leave a Kool-Aid Man–style hole in the wall. But a Catholic sees that and thinks, "Wow, I wonder if that sweaty blood could work miracles?!" Turns out, that's exactly what it did. The tomb of Charbel became a huge pilgrimage site, and the miracle goo flowed until the mid-twentieth century when the body finally decayed.

Saint Bernadette Soubirous a.k.a. Bernadette of Lourdes (1844–1879)

Bernadette became famous when, at the age of fourteen, she had a series of visions of the Virgin Mary near her home in Lourdes, France. During one of the visions, Mary told Bernadette to dig up a natural spring that would have healing powers. She did, and it did. The spring at Lourdes remains a hugely popular tourist attraction for Catholics hoping for a miracle or at least a nice trip to France. Despite being famous for literally digging up a healing spring, Bernadette died of illness at the age of thirty-five. When she was exhumed thirty years later, her body was incorrupt, even though her clothing and the rosary she was buried with were rusted and decayed. The sisters of her religious order bathed her, put her in fresh clothes, and reburied her. Bernadette was exhumed again in 1919 and found to still be incorrupt. But this time there was some discoloration to her face, which was blamed on the bath the sisters gave her, which seems kind of rude and scapegoat-y to the women who were nice enough to literally wash and dress a dead body. To protect the face from further decay, it was treated with a clear wax coating, in a sort of heavenly version of the food shellac used to preserve example sandwiches in the deli window. Bernadette's incorrupt-ish body is currently on display in a glass and gold case at the Chapel of Saint Bernadette in Nevers, France. There are plenty of good delis nearby.

Saint Andrew Bobola (1590–1657)

Andrew was martyred by the Cossacks, who at the time were trying to run the Jesuits out of Poland. And they did a thorough job. Andrew was beaten, dragged by horses, burned, strangled, flayed, and finally killed by a sword. This detail is important because it means Andrew's body was in pretty horrible condition when he died. That's why people were so shocked when, forty years after his death, his body was exhumed and found incorrupt. Beat the hell up, but still, incorrupt. But Andrew didn't get to rest in peace. He was exhumed multiple times and even briefly put on exhibit in a Russian museum in the early twentieth century. In the 1920s he was finally returned to the Vatican, where he was eventually examined by a team of doctors who deemed the condition of his body to be miraculous. This makes Andrew one of the few saints whose incorruption counts as one of his miracles toward canonization. His body is entombed at the Church of St. Andrew Bobola in Warsaw, Poland, thankfully not on view.

Saint Cuthbert (c. 634–687)

Cuthbert attempted the hermit life but was too darn popular and eventually got promoted to bishop. Roughly a decade after his death, he was exhumed and his body and clothing were found to be incorrupt. Due to constant invasions and battles, Cuthbert got exhumed a lot. He was moved in 875, 999, and 1104, when his body was discovered to be emitting a sweet fragrance. In 1537, Henry VIII, who was mad about the whole "I want to marry lots of women and the church keeps telling me no" thing, ordered the tomb plundered and body destroyed. However, the hired goons couldn't bring themselves to do it when they discovered the body fully intact and even with a little bit of five o'clock shadow. Cuthbert's beard-growing corpse was reinterred and left alone until 1827 when it was exhumed and found to contain only bones. So, to be considered incorrupt, you don't have to stay that way forever. Just long enough to be seen and maybe grow a little goatee.

Saints Who Were Virgins and Martyrs a.k.a. Virgin Martyrs

If Catholics love two things, it's dying like Christ and not having sex.[*] For those reasons, one of the most sacred types of saints is the virgin martyr. The virgin martyrs are young (often very young) women who died as retribution for resisting male advances. Some important things to keep in mind while reading these stories are that they are (a) tragic and (b) mostly fictional. It seems that, in order to create their ideal models of female purity, the Church had to embellish a teensy little gigantic bit.

The Catholic Catechism is pretty cut-and-dried when it comes to sex: it should be between a man and a woman, within the confines of marriage, for the purpose of having babies. Okay, technically it doesn't say "having babies"; it says "fecundity,"[†] which is maybe the least sexy word ever created. The point is, there's not a lot of wiggle room[‡] when it comes to sex.

There are enough of these stories that "virgin martyr" is often considered a subcategory of saints. These young (and again, often

---

[*] Or at least preaching about the importance of not having sex.
[†] Fun fact: The goal of sex for Catholics is largely procreative, but the Catechism calls out sperm and egg donation, surrogacy, and IVF as immoral. So much for fecundity!
[‡] For Catholics, "wiggle room" counts as sex.

fictional) ladies are meant to be models of purity for young Catholic women. You may notice a common thread in these stories: sex is portrayed as something done "to" women, and as an act of violence to be feared. Is that the best lesson to teach to young women? No. The best lesson to teach to young men? Also, no. But, is it a fair representation of the spectrum of human sexuality? Definitely not. You get the idea.

Here are some of the virgin martyrs.

Saint Agatha (d. c. 251)

You read about Agatha in the chapter "Saints Who Probably Joined Religious Orders to Avoid Shitty Marriages." Tit cakes? That's her. Agatha is also one of the virgin martyrs.

"Don't call me tit cakes." —Agatha

Saint Agnes of Rome (d. c. 304)

Not much is known about Agnes, other than she died after being betrayed as a Catholic to the Romans, possibly by a guy she rejected. One version of the story says that she was thrown into a brothel as punishment. Fortunately for Agnes, every man who attempted to touch her was instantly blinded. Blinding the patrons isn't great for business, so Agnes didn't last long at the brothel. According to most legends, she was eventually martyred by being raked over hot coals. Agnes is often depicted in art with a lamb because of the similarity to the Latin word for lamb (*agnus*) and her name. Also, because lambs are a symbol of purity and, oh yeah, all this happened when Agnes was TWELVE FREAKING YEARS OLD.*

Saint Barbara (d. Late Third or Early Fourth Century)

Along with Saint Christopher, Barbara is one of the saints who was removed from the liturgical calendar in 1969 due to a serious case of not being real. But she is still revered as a virgin martyr thanks to her inspirational and deeply insane story. According to legend, Barbara was the beautiful daughter of a wealthy, pagan family. Her father made her live in a high tower to protect her from all the princes who came by asking for her hand in marriage. At this point, Barbara is basically Rapunzel, except instead of long hair, Barbara had a secret devotion to Christ. One day, while her father was away, Barbara snuck down from her tower to get baptized. When daddy returned home and found out she was Catholic,

---

* Some sources say she might have been as old as fifteen, so, ancient.

he became enraged and turned her in to the authorities. Barbara was ultimately martyred by her own father, which is sad. But then God immediately sought justice by frying her dad with a bolt of lightning, which is pretty awesome.

Saint Dymphna (Seventh Century Maybe?)

There are no historical records of Saint Dymphna's life, but there is a hell of a story. According to legend, Dymphna was the beautiful daughter of doting, wealthy parents.

"Who's ready for potluck? I brought the tiny building!" —Barbara

Her father was a pagan, but her mother was a Christian and raised Dymphna to be extremely religious. It was a happy childhood until Dymphna's mother died. Fortunately, her dad decided to remarry. Unfortunately, the bride he picked was his own daughter. Dymphna was understandably not a fan of this idea, so she fled with a priest. Dymphna's dad tracked her and the priest down and beheaded them both. One version of the legend says Dymphna and the priest also fled with the court jester and his wife, who seem to have survived. So, if there is any truth the legend of Dymphna, it seems likely we have a comedian to thank.

Saint Lucy (d. 304)

Little is known for sure about Lucy because—say it with me—she may not have been real. The most accepted version of her story says that she was born to wealthy parents and decided she wanted to remain a virgin and devote herself to Christ at a young age. Unfortunately, Lucy's parents didn't get the memo soon enough, and her mother had already agreed to marry her off to a young man. When Lucy rejected the man, he—say it with me—fell into a murderous rage. Since being a Christian was illegal at this point, the groom-not-to-be turned Lucy over to the authorities, and she was tortured and sentenced to work as a prostitute. This is where the story splits. In one version, authorities blinded her but then God restored her sight. In another version, Lucy plucked out her own eyes and presented them on a tray to her suitor to dissuade him from marrying her. You've got to hand it to Lucy, eyeballs on a tray is definitely a turnoff.

"Hey. Eyes down here, buddy."
—Lucy

Saint Margaret of Antioch (d. c. 304)

Margaret is one of the many saints who was removed from the official Catholic calendar of saints for being a little fictional. Her story is pretty similar to the other virgin martyrs: a young woman, lusted after by a man, refuses his advances and gets reported to the authorities for being Christian. What makes Margaret's story different is how many people she took down with her. Legend says that Margaret was publicly tortured by being immersed in boiling water and, when she survived, the crowd was so moved that hundreds of them converted on the spot. Maybe they should've waited until they got home, because, due to the whole "Christianity is illegal" thing, the fresh converts were immediately arrested and executed. When Margaret was finally successfully killed by beheading, her executioner instantly fell dead at her feet. Margaret comes in with a death toll of allegedly about a thousand, making her the John Wick of virgin martyrs.

Saints Who Were Nepo Babies

As with most things in life, when it comes to sainthood, it helps to be born on third base. Canonization takes time, effort, and a certain amount of fame, all of which come a little easier when mommy and/or daddy did it first.

These saints absolutely worked hard to earn their halos, but it's hard not to notice the extra help they had along the way. If you want to increase your odds of making it into the Ivy League of heaven, here are some folks you might want to emulate.

Saint Adalbald of Ostrevant (d. c. 650–652)

Saint Adalbald was a martyr, which made him a shoo-in for sainthood. But it didn't hurt that his mom was Saint Gertrude of Hamage.* The connections didn't stop there. Adalbald's wife was Saint Rictrude, and all four of his children—Maurontius, Clotsindis, Eusebia, and Adalsindis—became saints. Adalbald's family members weren't all models of holiness. In fact, his wife's family never liked him and actually had him assassinated. Keep that in mind the next time you complain about your in-laws at Thanksgiving.

Saint Anne (n.d.)

Anne is a unique case because she wasn't born of a saint, but her grandson was—drumroll please—JESUS FREAKING CHRIST. Here's the backstory: mourning their inability to conceive, Anne's husband Joachim left to spend forty days in the desert praying for a child. Spending over a month away from your wife is typically not the best solution for infertility, but the prayers seem to have worked, because an angel appeared to Anne and told her they would conceive. Joachim returned home and he and Anne embraced at the gates of Jerusalem. Must've been one helluva hug, because nine months later, Anne gave birth to Mary, who eventually gave birth to Jesus, making Anne the first nepo nana.

---

* Accounts also say she might have been his grandmother, which means Gertrude let him get away with either nothing or everything.

Saint Basil the Great (c. 329–379)

Some men are born great, and that definitely applies to Saint Basil. Not only were both of Basil's parents—Basil the Elder and Emmelia—saints, so were three of his nine siblings: Saint Macrina, Saint Gregory of Nyssa, and Saint Peter of Sabaste. Plus, his grandmother was Saint Macrina the Elder. You know your family is holy when you have enough saints to field a bobsled team, including alternates.

"What do you mean, 'smile'? This is my smile."
—Basil the Great

Saint Gregory of Nazianzus the Younger (c. 325–389 or 390)

Gregory's parents were Saint Nonna and Saint Gregory of Nazianzus the Elder, and his siblings were Saint Gorgonia and Saint Caesarius. As if being a saint wasn't enough of an advantage, Greg the Elder was also bishop of Nazianzus, which meant he was able to send his son to study at some of the best schools in the world. It was at one of those top schools where lil' Greg met his best bud Basil a.k.a. the previously mentioned Saint Basil the Great. Greg absolutely worked hard, but it's difficult to guess what his life would've been like if he'd had to work three jobs to put himself through Ancient Athens Community College.

> **DOCTOR OF THE CHURCH**
>
> An honorary title given to saints who have made significant contributions to the theological teachings of the Church, like Saint Augustine, Saint Jerome, and Saint Basil the Great. So, the next time your parents pressure you to become a doctor say, "How about a doctor...of the Church?!" and watch the disappointment grow in their weary eyes.

Nepo Baby Saint Subcategory: Royalty

The following saints don't have holy parents, but they have a special distinction because they are the original nepo babies: monarchs. These saints all did impressive, virtuous things in life, but they also had castles, so take their accomplishments with a grain of salt.

Saint Stephen of Hungary (c. 970–1038)

Stephen is the patron saint of Hungary and used his Christianity as a tool to unite his people and protect his nation. And he took it seriously. During his reign, Stephen built a cathedral, divided his nation into dioceses, made tithing mandatory, required marriage (unless you had a religious vocation), and decreed that any couple with more than ten children had to send the tenth kid off to a monastery. Sounds rough, but so does having ten kids before the invention of the epidural. Stephen's son Emeric could be considered a saint nepo baby because he has also been canonized. Unfortunately, Emeric didn't benefit from royal nepotism since he was killed by a wild boar during a hunting accident before he had a chance to ascend the throne. Still doesn't sound as bad as ten natural labors.

Saint Edward the Confessor (1004–1066)

Saint Edward is called "the confessor" to denote that he lived a virtuous life but did not die a martyr. Plus, that name was already taken by Saint Edward the Martyr (who was also a relative, making Edward the Confessor a double nepo baby). Edward not-the-Martyr became king around the age of forty and ruled with the energy of a middle-aged man. His reign was relatively conflict-free, and he seems to have spent his time doing the middle-ages equivalent of tinkering around in the garage: building and renovating churches, including what is now the famous Westminster Abbey. Edward and his wife, Edith, lived celibate lives and left no heirs, which is great for a saint but really kind of the main job of a monarch.

> **CONFESSOR**
>
> Confessors are saints who suffered like Christ but weren't martyred. So, if you get tortured, imprisoned, exiled, and generally take a lot of shit for professing your faith—everything short of being killed—you're a confessor. Also, probably not a ton of fun at parties.

Saint Louis IX (1214–1270)

"Why choose between sword and pointy stick when you can have both!" —Louis IX

Louis IX was crowned king of France at the age of twelve, so it wouldn't have been shocking if he'd grown up to be a privileged jerk. Luckily, his mom, Queen Blanche, took the lead until little Louis came of age. When he did take over, he hit the ground running. His diverse resume includes building a monastery, supporting religious orders, collecting religious relics from across the world, and building a home for reformed prostitutes and a hospital for the blind. Unfortunately for Louis, he shot a little too close to the sun when he kicked off not one, but two crusades. Louis's crusades could be described with two words: expensive and unsuccessful. The first ended in King Louis IX being kidnapped, and the second in him dying of scurvy.[*] It's a sad end to a long and impressive life, but it was all worth it because it earned him a halo and a spot as the namesake of St. Louis, Missouri.

Saint Oswald (d. 642)

Oswald was king of Northumbria (an area that is now parts of northern England and southern Scotland) and is another double nepo baby,

---

[*] It also could've been plague or dysentery. Louis never would've survived the game *The Oregon Trail*.

because he was the nephew of Saint Edwin, who was also once king of Northumbria. Like his saint/king/uncle, Oswald was a convert and made sure people knew it: he built churches and monasteries, donated generously to the poor, and is even said to have erected a cross on a battlefield with his own two hands. He probably should've erected a fort instead, because he was killed in battle in 642.

HONORABLE NEPO MENTION

Worth including because good gossip never gets old.

Saint Innocent I (unknown–417)

Innocent I was pope from 401 to 417, succeeding Pope Anastasius I. Innocent ran a tight ship and was especially strict about clerical celibacy, which is a little ironic because there is speculation that he was actually the son of Pope Anastasius I. Nobody knows the truth for sure, but typically "pope" isn't a job that's supposed to be passed from father to son.

STEP 1 COMPLETE!
Achievement Unlocked: Corpse

THE PROS:

- You no longer have to worry about when and how you might die, because you did.
- You have no more bills to pay.
- You don't have to pretend you have food poisoning to get out of work which, to any bosses who might be reading this, none of us have ever done.

THE CONS:

- You're dead.

WHAT THE HELL IS A HALO?

f you've ever seen a painting of a saint, you know the official badge of sainthood is a halo. It's the round disk of light that emanates from behind the head of a saint. Halos are about both fashion and function. Like umbrellas used by tour guides, halos are a useful tool for picking out saints in a crowd.

But what the hell is a halo? If being a saint makes rays of light shoot out of your head, why does it only happen after people die and go to heaven? It would be way more helpful if saints had halos while here on Earth. They'd be easier to spot, and they could help you find your car keys at the bottom of your purse at night.

Also, why the head? There's

"There she is." —the guys without halos

nothing uniquely holy about our heads. Why not have rays of light shoot out of our hearts? Or eyes? Or livers? Or out of our fingertips and toes like Beast at the end of *Beauty and the Beast*?[*] One logical theory is that the halo was meant to mimic the symbolism of crowns. Another is that halos were designed to act as wide-brimmed hats and protect statues of holy figures from bird droppings. That theory is less logical but definitely more fun.

Turns out, like so many things in Catholicism (the dates of Christmas and Easter and the existence of guardian angels, to name a few), halos were an idea swiped from someone else. Early Greek and Roman art often portrayed gods or powerful figures with halos or rays of light behind them.[†] The earliest known instance of the traditional disc halo is from Iran around 300 BCE. Christianity adopted the visual cue around the fourth century, at first just in depictions of Jesus, to indicate that he was a major player on the world religions scene. Eventually, the halo fad had caught on, and everyone from angels to saints to apostles got one.

There were some halo fads that didn't take off. In the early

"I feel stupid." —Pope John VII

---

[*] To fully appreciate this joke, please pause here and watch the entire 1991 animated Disney classic *Beauty and the Beast*. Not the live action remake, you heathen.
[†] They were also used in ancient Buddhist and Hindu art, because everybody looks good with their own spotlight!

Middle Ages, powerful clergy or influential donors were occasionally depicted in art with square halos. This didn't catch on, for obvious reasons.

The use of halos in art even played a role in the evolution of the canonization process itself. For most of church history, the title of "blessed" was thrown around pretty loosely. It wasn't until the 1400s that the Vatican made official distinctions between people who were beatified and people who were fully canonized. It sounds like a technicality, but this was a solid concession to local dicasteries who were eager to

"You guys! The email said we were all wearing bucket hats!"
—the doofus in the bucket hat

worship their local holy folks and understandably getting impatient with the glacial speed of canonization. The pope couldn't risk another Great/Western/Great Western Schism, so boom: beatification!

Beatified people, known as blesseds, are holy enough to be venerated at the local level, but not yet fully recognized as saints. Church leaders came up with a clever art hack to keep everyone happy and haloed: beatified people could be portrayed with rays coming out of their head, while saints got a fully saturated halo. Then, if the beatified person ever got fully canonized, it was easy enough to go back in with a paintbrush and fill in between the rays to upgrade them.

Everybody won, except for the people with square halos, who were sadly stuck looking dumb for eternity.

As both Catholicism and art evolved over time, so did halos. Jesus and Mary are often depicted with an aureole or mandorla, which is an almond-shaped halo behind their entire body. God gets a special type of halo, and so does Jesus. To keep it all straight, here's a quick halo guide that you can cut out and take with you the next time you're in heaven/at an art museum.

Quick Halo Guide

SQUARE: For powerful clergy like popes and bishops. Also for rich donors who funded the construction of churches. That's why some figures are depicted holding tiny churches. Bonus non-halo fact!

RAYS: Typically for beatified people a.k.a. blessed a.k.a. almost-but-not-quite saints. Can easily be filled in and made into a regular disc halo if they reach sainthood.

CIRCLE: Saints. Sometimes God and Jesus—and Buddha, various Hindu figures, Apollo, and Poseidon because, again, Christianity didn't invent halos.

TRIANGLE: God only. Represents the Holy Trinity (God the Father, Jesus the Son, and the Holy Spirit, who's really their own thing).

CRUCIFORM HALO: Jesus. Represents the Holy Trinity. Everybody in the Trinity gets a special halo except for the Holy Spirit, who is usually depicted as a ray of light. Putting a halo on a ray of light is too matchy-matchy.

AUREOLE/MANDORLA: Full-body halo for Jesus and Mary to show that they are extra super holy.

CIRCULAR HALO OF STARS: Mary when depicted as the Woman of the Apocalypse, who is described in the Book of Revelation as wearing a crown of twelve stars. Also, Mary as depicted when you hang an EU flag behind her.

CIRCLE WITH AN X THROUGH IT: Do not dry clean.

STEP 2
Have Your Whole Life Investigated

t this point, you're dead, which means you're off to a great start! Hopefully, you were either a good person or smart enough to avoid social media, because Step 2 involves a team of researchers investigating every nook and cranny of your life. Now is when the real work begins (for other people—remember you're dead).

If you were martyred, this step isn't so bad. Dying like Christ is considered the ultimate Christian sacrifice, so martyrs get more of a pass on sins. As long as researchers can prove you were killed because of your faith, this step is easy peasy lemon squeezy.[*] But, if you were one of those poor unfortunate souls who lived a long, fulfilling life, it's a little harder.

To kick off the process, someone from your local community, usually called the "petitioner," needs to reach out to the local bishop and say that you seem worthy of canonization. If the bishop agrees with the petitioner, he reaches out to the other bishops in his area

---

[*] Lemon squeezy, by the way, is a horrible way to get martyred.

to see if they're on board. As long as the bishops are cool with it, your journey to canonization, now called the "cause," is officially opened. Just like that, you've earned your first new title: Servant of God. Congrats! Treat yourself to an espresso martini or whatever is trendy in heaven right now.

If you have any skeletons in your closet, now is when they'll come out. The bishop will appoint someone to begin the assignment of gathering everything you've ever written, read, said, and done. This person is known as the "postulator" and will stay with your cause all the way to the end. The postulator is the most important person tied to your canonization cause other than you. Postulators are the ones in direct contact with Church officials; they coordinate any additional needed staff, assemble all the research on your life, oversee the accounting, and make sure all the canon laws are followed to a T.[†] So, you'd better hope you get a good one. And one with some flexibility, because the postulator actually has to move to Rome for the second half of your canonization process.

Depending on how much information you left behind and how long ago you lived, this part of the process alone could take decades. In fact, many postulators who start the canonization process assume they won't live long enough to see their candidate become a saint. On the bright side, dying before the canonization process is surefire way to find out if your candidate made it to heaven!

In addition to compiling everything you ever said or wrote, officials

---

[†] Church rules also stipulate that the postulator can be no older than eighty, which is a great idea that maybe the U.S. Congress should consider!

need to interview people who personally knew you. That process is supervised by someone called the promoter of justice. In addition to having the best title in all of Catholicism, the promoter of justice is in charge of making sure your journey to sainthood process follows canon law. Also, all those interviews need to be notarized, so maybe do them at a UPS Store.*

The goal of this phase is to gather evidence proving that you lived a life of heroic virtue. The Catholic virtues are faith, hope, charity, prudence, justice, fortitude, and temperance. To practice those to a heroic degree means going above and beyond. For example, where the average Catholic would set up an auto-donation to the ASPCA,† you would open your home to stray animals. Bad for the floors, good for your future halo.

> **DEVIL'S ADVOCATE**
>
> This used to be the person at the Vatican in charge of questioning a saint's cause. They were responsible for finding any faults in the case and ensuring that only iron-clad causes were advanced to the pontiff. This was great in theory but often kept causes tied up for decades. That's a big reason why Pope John Paul II got rid of the position in 1983. It was a win for speedier canonizations but a huge blow to cool Vatican job titles.

---

* Or most banks. Wow! So much information in this book!
† Do it! They send you a free calendar with pictures of cute animals!

This step is also when your team will start collecting relics: objects that were important to you in life, including your now hopefully dead body. Your team also needs to see if there are any signs of incorruptibility on your body, so a representative from your diocese, possibly the bishop, will visit your tomb to make sure everything is in order. Hopefully, they go at night with a flashlight for a spooky good time.

Once every teensy little detail about your life has been gathered, collated, and triple-checked, it is compiled into a document called an *Acta*. As long as the *Acta* meets the satisfaction of the bishop and local clergy, it gets photocopied, packed up, and sent off to the Vatican for review by the official saint makers over at the Dicastery for the Causes of Saints. Grab your passport and your gelato-eating pants, because your cause is headed to Rome!

STEP 2: CHECKLIST
- ✓ Live a life of heroic virtue.
- ✓ Leave behind evidence that you lived a life of heroic virtue.
- ✓ Don't make a lot of enemies (or just make sure they die before you).
- ✓ Make sure your bishop likes you.

The Heroic Virtues

There are seven virtues in Catholicism: faith, hope, charity, prudence, justice, fortitude, and temperance. Every Catholic is supposed to practice these virtues in everyday life, but saints are expected to raise the bar. Then avoid the bar. That's kind of the whole deal behind temperance.

Because nothing can be simple in Catholicism, the heroic virtues are split into two categories. The first three (faith, hope, and charity) are called the theological virtues because they are related directly to God. Theological virtues are what distinguish between a regular good person and a Catholic good person. The last four (prudence, justice, fortitude, and temperance) are the cardinal virtues because they are the basic things every human should do to be a good member of society regardless of their religion. The cardinal virtues are also in their own separate category because they are actually attributed to Plato, who came up with them about four hundred years before Christianity existed.[*]

Now, "heroic" is a pretty intimidating word, and between work, errands, and picking the kids up from basketball,[†] it can be hard to find time to focus on virtues. But don't worry, it's easy to squeeze the heroic virtues into everyday life.

FAITH means you believe in God and all the teachings of the Church, regardless of proof. To Catholics, the existence of God isn't opinion, it's fact. Faith can be expressed by:
- Living in accordance with scripture
- Observing the Ten Commandments
- Ordering Taco Bell on a night you know you're going to have

---

[*] Honestly, it's on Plato for not also inventing the concept of plagiarism.
[†] You're late!!!

sex. There's no proof that this will end well for anyone, so you'll have to rely on faith!

If faith means you believe in heaven, then **HOPE** means you *reeeaaaally* want to go there. Hope is the desire to be reunited with God and achieve everlasting life. Hope can be expressed by:

- Praying regularly
- Performing random acts of kindness
- Being a Cleveland Browns fan

CHARITY means demonstrating your love for God by showing love for your fellow man. It can be expressed by:

- Spending time with the lonely
- Donating money or resources to the poor
- Saying "You have it, I'm full" about the last piece of pizza in the fridge even though you wanted that piece so freaking bad

PRUDENCE means making good decisions. You can express prudence by:

- Consulting religious texts or leaders before making big decisions
- Focusing on work before pleasure
- Not getting wasted on your wedding night. Do something classier, like getting wasted on your honeymoon.

JUSTICE means giving God and people what they are owed. Justice can be expressed by:

- Giving back unearned or stolen money

- Negotiating fairly for goods or services
- Becoming Batman

FORTITUDE is the ability to continue doing what is right despite fear or outside pressure. It can be expressed by:

- Continuing with a job or schoolwork even when it gets hard
- Speaking up against bullies
- Not buying the big claw clip. It will give you a headache. It'll be uncomfortable to wear while driving. It'll never look as cute as you think it will. You *know* this. It doesn't matter that big claw clips are trending again. Stay strong. DON'T BUY THE BIG CLAW CLIP.

TEMPERANCE is the ability to control yourself when faced with desire. Temperance can be expressed by:

- Not overindulging in alcohol or drugs
- Staying faithful to your partner if monogamous
- Not eating raw cookie dough[*]

Quick Tips

Anyone who lived a life of heroic virtue and/or was martyred technically has an equal shot of becoming a saint. But by now, you've probably noticed that canonization isn't exactly a meritocracy. These quick tips may just help bump you up to heaven's captain's table.

---

[*] Okay. Not eating *as much* raw cookie dough. You're a saint, not a god.

1. **Be a pope.** As the Official Holiest Guys on Earth, popes have a leg up when it comes to canonization. In fact, fifty-two of the first fifty-five popes became saints. Sucks for those other three guys. Sadly, women aren't allowed to be pope, so this tip only works for the fellas.
2. **Be a priest or a nun.** Your odds of becoming pope are slim, but almost anyone can become a priest or nun. This is a perk because (a) your whole day job is being virtuous and (b) holy orders have built-in machinery to support causes. It's way easier to advance a cause of sainthood when you already have connections at the Vatican. Is this fair? Probably not. But the vast majority of saints are priests, nuns, and popes, so you might as well give it a shot.
3. **Don't be married.** Less than 10 percent of saints were married. If you're wondering why, see the previous two tips.
4. **Be Italian.** A lot of saints are Italian. How much is a lot? We're talking almost 50 percent of all saints as of 2010. Also, they have pasta and wine. Becoming Italian is really a win no matter how you look at it.

Saints Who Could Kick Your Ass

Given the importance of the heroic virtues, you'd think killing lots of people would be an immediate disqualifier for sainthood, but you'd be wrong! Catholics are far from perfect, and the canon of saints is full of folks who bashed a few heads on their way to heaven. Everyone loves a sinner-to-saint story, and these people had the "sinner" part down.

As you figure out what kind of saint you want to be, just remember: violence is never the answer, unless God tells you it is, in which case, go kick some ass.

Saint Olga (c. 890–969)

Body count: hundreds, maybe thousands

Technically, Olga was queen of an area in Eastern Europe known as Kievan Rus. More accurately, she was the queen of revenge. Shortly after becoming king, Olga's husband, Igor, was murdered by a tribe called the Drevlians. Hoping to spin the whole "we murdered your husband" thing into a positive, the Drevlians sent an envoy to Olga, suggesting she marry the prince of the Drevlians and unite their tribes. Olga played nice and said she'd think about the offer and give them her answer in the morning. Her answer? The next morning, she had her guards throw the entire envoy into a giant pit and bury them alive. But Olga wasn't done. She sent a messenger to the Drevlians saying she was interested in the proposal but wanted them to send a group of escorts to bring her to them. Pumped that things were going so well, the Drevlians sent their best to Olga. This time, when they arrived, Olga invited them to use the bathhouse to freshen up. Once the Drevlian envoy was inside, she locked the doors and set the building on fire. At this point you might be thinking, *Wow, that's a lot of killing for a saint!* But Olga wasn't done yet. She again reached out to the Drevlians and said she was ready to get re-hitched but needed to bury her husband first. She asked that the Drevlian prince and his entourage attend and pay their respects. Instead of replying, "Hey, quick Q: How come nobody we sent your way has come home yet?" the

Drevlians said, "Cool! On our way!" They attended the funeral and the booze-filled after-party. Once the Drevlians were sufficiently drunk, Olga ordered her guards to kill them all. To button everything up, Olga then marched with her troops to the Drevlian city, burned it down, and sold any survivors into slavery. Anyway, a few years later, Olga converted to Christianity, built a bunch of churches, and eventually became a saint. She never remarried, perhaps because she was terrifying. So, if you're concerned your sinful past will prohibit you from becoming a saint, don't worry about it. Olga is proof you can be a *Game of Thrones*–level destroyer of cities and still end up with a halo!

"I've been told I have resting murder face." —Olga

Saint Vladimir (956–1015)

Body count: dozens (conservative estimate)

Vladimir was Olga's grandson, and the apple doesn't fall far from the murderer. Vladimir was the illegitimate child of Olga's son Svyatoslav. When King Daddy died, the crown was handed over to Vladimir's legit brother, Yaropolk. Vladimir wasn't a fan of this plan, so he deposed his brother, had him assassinated, and then forced his sister-in-law to join his massive harem. Vladimir also practiced human sacrifice.

He was a real Renaissance man of bad stuff. After amassing tons of power (and concubines), Vladimir had a chance to marry a Byzantine princess on one condition: he convert to Christianity. To everyone's shock (especially the concubines'), Vladimir took his conversion very seriously. He became monogamous, converted many of his countrymen, built churches, donated to the poor, and abolished the death penalty in his kingdom—a little late for his former human sacrifices.

Joan of Arc (1412–1431)

Body count: hundreds

Joan became famous for leading the French army to victory in Orleans in 1429 at the age of seventeen. Despite being a young woman who couldn't read or write and had zero military training, Joan did what generations of soldiers before her had failed to do: beat the English. Thanks in large parts to her efforts, Charles VII was crowned king of France. As thanks, he offered Joan—who had been injured in battle—and her family a place in the French court and a shot at the good life. Unfortunately, Joan tried to press her luck and returned to battle. Evidently the whole "I don't need military training because God sent me" thing was a one-time deal. Joan and her troops were defeated, and Joan was captured by the English. Turns out King Charles was more like Jerk Charles, because he did nothing to barter for Joan's release. She was found guilty of heresy and burned at the stake at the age of nineteen. Twenty-five years after her death, the Church officially reversed its decision and declared her a very much notheretic. She is now a patron saint of soldiers and France. Sadly for Chuck, there is no patron saint of ungrateful kings.

> **HERESY**
>
> Any belief that goes against the accepted doctrine of a religion. For example, believing that Jesus and God are totally separate entities instead of one in the Holy Trinity would be an act of heresy. Heresy typically refers to religion, but it can also pertain to secular beliefs. For example: fruit on pizza is an act of heresy.

Saint Michael the Archangel (All Time)

Body count: lots, but mostly other angels

Michael is an angel, but he's not just any angel, he's God's head warrior. When Satan and his army tried to revolt against God, it was Michael who led his own army of angels to victory, sending Satan and his forces to hell. Michael is also one of the saints who appeared to Joan of Arc in visions when she was a child, telling her to take up arms for France. So, he's kind of a bad influence. Michael is invoked as a defender of the faith and has a side gig guarding the gates of purgatory. Leader of God's army to bouncer seems like a bit of a demotion, but if you make it to heaven, maybe don't say that to his face. He has a huge sword.

Saints Who It Turns Out Probably Weren't Real

Ahoy matey! 'Tis I, Saint Christopher, patron saint of travelers. And I be knowin' what ye be thinkin': *Who does this bilge-suckin' son of a biscuit eater think he is? Saint Christopher weren't no pirate!* To that I say: How can ye prove I wasn't? I weren't real!

Here's the scuttlebutt: Legend says a buccaneer named Christopher (that be me) came across a child needin' to cross a wee bit-o-water. I heaved ho and lifted the child onto m'shoulders swifter than a whore's legs o'er her head, then carried the lad across the briny deep, keepin' him safe all the while. When we got to the other side the whippersnapper proclaimed that he was none other than the Christ child. I went on to convert thousands of scalawags to Christianity and was martyred by beheading after forty archers failed to knick a hair on m'noggin'. Oh also, one time, the Christ child blessed me walkin' stick, so I planted it in the dirt and, shiver me timbers, the next day it was a palm tree.

'Tis a whale of a tale! And as real as an itch on a peg leg. Turns out at best I might have been based on a real seadog named Kester who died around 251 in Asia Minor. The rest be hornswaggle and cackle tassel! And I ain't the only freebooter in the bunch: Saint Veronica, Saint Margaret of Antioch, Saint Philomena, Saint Barbara, Saint Eustace, and Saint George are all as true as a sailor's vow of monogamy. For feck's sake, two of 'em have dragons in their stories. A bit of a giveaway, I be thinkin'.

"'Okay, in hindsight the water weren't that deep." —Christopher

That's why, in 1969, Pope No-Fun-Scurvy-Dog kicked me off the official liturgical calendar and sent me feast day to Davy Jones's locker. But I get to keep me halo and me sainthood for one very important technical reason: I be popular! Givin' the ole Christ child a piggyback ride makes me the patron saint of travelers. 'Tis why every Catholic worth their salt has a medal to ole Chris in their car.

Let this be a lesson to all you long-clothed bilge rats who want to sail through the Pearly Gates: A saint is only as good as their story. So make yours a good one. Savvy?

> **HAGIOGRAPHY**
>
> A hagiography is a biography of a saint or a saint-to-be. Since the whole point of writing a hagiography is to pump up the popularity of the subject, they're usually pretty flattering. Think of hagiographies like dating profiles for saints. They're less "tell-all" and more "tell-some-make-a-little-up-if-you-have-to."

The Saint Sex Talk

The Catholic Church is not what most people would describe as "sex positive." Jesus was born to a virgin, priests and nuns take vows of celibacy, and you're expected to wait until marriage to have sex.* Also,

---

*   Heterosexual marriage. Because, as it definitely doesn't say in The First Letter to the Corinthians, "Love is patient, love is kind, love is straight and totally not gay."

no masturbating ever. And no pornography. Basically, for a good time, don't call the Catholic Church.

Historically, the Church has had a hard time squaring sexual activity with sainthood, especially when it comes to women, nonbinary people, transgender people, and members of the LGBTQ+ community. Official church teaching is that sex is primarily procreative, not recreational, and should be reserved for marriage. But marriage also puts you at a disadvantage, because less than 10 percent of saints were married. So, if you want to be canonized, you may need to reevaluate your sex life. Aspiring saints basically have two options: have lots of sex and then repent for it, or never have sex ever at all. Wanting to bump halos is natural, so break out the bananas and condoms,[*] because it's time for a sex talk from the saints themselves.

Saint Augustine of Hippo (354–430)

"Hey champ, plop a squat. I hear you've started to show a little interest in, uh, downstairs activity. I want you to know it's totally natural and also bad, but everyone does it, so don't do it. Okay? Lemme back up. I was a little wild in my youth. I had sex and went to plays, which we all know are the sex of the brain. I even took a mistress and had a son. But then I realized the error of my ways. I needed to find a good, solid woman to marry. And I couldn't marry my mistress—she was a mistress! So, I did the right thing: gave the woman who loved me and bore me a son the boot and agreed to marry a twelve-year-old child.

---

[*] And then put them away because most contraception is also against church rules. Ask your grandparents about the rhythm method.

Don't worry, I didn't actually marry the woman (again, in this case 'woman' means 'twelve-year-old child'), because I ended up deciding to become a monk and lived out the rest of my days in celibacy. I also wrote a super-famous book called *Confessions* where I talk about my awesome sinful life and how it was very cool but wrong. So don't have sex, but if you do, have a ton, then write a book about how bad you feel about it. Got it? Good talk."

"Heads up, God! Hot potato!" —Augustine

Saint Ursula (Fourth or Fifth Century?)

"What's up, kiddo? It's your cool aunt, Saint Ursula. When it comes to virgin martyrs, I am legendary, and I do mean that literally because I was not real. Here's my deal: My dad wanted to marry me off to a pagan prince, and I was like, 'No thank you.' But he was like, 'You're a woman, you don't get to say no,' and I was like, 'Oh right, it's the Middle Ages, that sucks.' Anyway, I talked him into letting me postpone the wedding while I went on a little vacay with my ten ladies in waiting and one thousand maidens. Some stories say it was actually eleven thousand maidens, but who's counting? Me and the ladies sailed all the way to Rome and had a freaking blast until we were either captured and massacred or shipwrecked and enslaved, depending on who you ask. Point is, if you want to have sex, that's fine. If you don't, just grab eleven thousand of your closest virgins and go die at sea. Got it? Cool talk."

> **PAGAN**
>
> A pagan can be someone who is polytheist (believes in more than one god) or worships nature. Historically, "pagan" has been used as a derogatory term for anyone whose religion isn't the dominant one, which is not a very nice thing to do, but you've probably noticed by now that the history of religion involves a lot of people doing not-so-nice things.

Saint Lucy (d. 304)

"Okay, before you roll your eyes, let me just say that being a virgin martyr is pretty cool. I know sex is fun and fulfilling and healthy and… what were we talking about? Oh right, never having sex and then dying! See, I always knew I wanted to consecrate myself to God. Unfortunately, I was already betrothed to a young man. When I broke the news to him, he turned me in for being Catholic (which was illegal in those days). I was sentenced to life as a prostitute (love an ironic punishment), but when they came to drag me away, my body became immovably heavy. Even a team of oxen couldn't get me to budge. They tried to set me on fire, I plucked out my own eyes, it was a whole thing. Anyway, they finally settled on thrusting a sword into my throat (that one took). What matters is that I stayed a virgin, and the symbolism of my demise coming from penetration by a phallic symbol is coincidence, I'm sure! Good talk!"

Saint Mary of Egypt (c. 344–c. 421)

"Come here, honey. Sit down. Plenty of saints have sex, and I am a saint who had plenty. I ran away to Alexandria when I was twelve and found my passion: fucking. Don't get it twisted; I wasn't a prostitute. It was never about money; it was about love of the game. I spent seventeen years doing everything and everyone in Egypt. Then one day while hanging out at the docks I saw a departing ship of pilgrims, so I went on board and banged. Every. Pilgrim. They wanted to see God, and baby, they did! When we landed, I followed my hot lil' pilgrims to church and converted on the spot. I spent the next forty-seven years wandering naked in the desert as a hermit. Take it from me, anyone can make it to sainthood if they repent hard enough. So go fuck a cruise ship, baby!"

Saint Andrew (d. 60)

"Look kid. You want a sex talk from a saint? Listen up. I was one of the Twelve Apostles. My brother was Saint Peter, the first pope. I was friends with Jesus and traveled preaching his word after

"Guys, how many times do I have to tell you: stop making the crucifixions look so sexy!" —the soldier with the poofy helmet

his death, but the thing I'm most famous for today is Saint Andrew's Cross, the X-shaped cross on which I was killed. You might recognize it as the flag of Scotland. Or because it's a popular piece of fucking BDSM equipment. That's right. I was *crucified* and somebody looked at my cross and thought, *Huh, bet I could get my rocks off on that*. You do you, kid. Just don't fucking fuck on my cross, okay? Fuck."

STEP 2 COMPLETE!

Achievement Unlocked: Servant of God

THE PROS:

- You have your first official title. Time to update your LinkedIn!
- Your postulator is going to Rome, which is fun for them but doesn't really matter to you since you're in heaven.
- The investigation into your life didn't turn up anything embarrassing, which is honestly huge. It's tough to be squeaky-clean post-internet.

THE CONS:

- Servant of God is the entry-level job for saints. Don't get stuck here, or you'll spend eternity getting coffees for the apostles.

DRESS FOR THE JOB YOU WANT

If you want to be a saint, you need to look the part. Luckily, there are plenty of images of saints throughout history to provide some much-needed fashion inspo.

Granduca Madonna

Raphael, 1506–1507

The ultimate fashionista is the Mother of God herself: the Madonna. Empire waists are very forgiving, just like the God who impregnated her with this chunky baby when she was only a teenager. As a bonus, this drapey veil/cape situation easily transitions from day to night to day again—useful considering it's probably the only outfit she owned.

Saint Quentin

Jacopo Pontormo, 1517–1518

Quentin is absolutely feeling himself in this understated beach look. The coral wrap says, "I'm comfy yet confident," while the spikes under his fingernails say, "Help! I'm being tortured by the Roman government!"

Saint Michael

Raphael, 1504–1505

Unrealistic body standards are a real issue in fashion, so it's understandable if you look at Michael and think, *Sure, he looks good in wings, but he's an archangel!* Don't be fooled—this ensemble can work for any body type. Just throw on a blue skirt, grab your best shield and sword combo, then go out there and slay... the Devil, as portrayed by a dragon.

Santa Teresa de Jesús

Eduardo Balaca, c. 1877

Take it from Saint Teresa of Avila: not every look needs to be complicated. Some days call for neutral tones and chill, yet pious vibes. Try this relaxed habit and cape look and finish it off with a flourish by summoning a dove to fly near your head at all times.

Joan of Arc at the Coronation of Charles VII in Reims Cathedral

Jean-Auguste-Dominque Ingres, 1854

Every outfit makes a statement, and this one says, "In the name of God and France, I will slay the English army." Joan of Arc rocks a monochromatic color scheme of metal on metal with a little bit of skirt, which, while impractical for the battlefield, really dresses up an otherwise casual 'fit. And of course, no "soldier of God" look is complete without a sword.

STEP 3

Have Your Whole Life Investigated Again but by People in Rome This Time

You've made it through the first two steps of canonization and officially became a Servant of God, so you're off to the races! Now you just have a few quick decades (or centuries) left to go. Luckily, you're dead—you've got time! The third step of canonization is basically the same as the second but done by a group called the Dicastery for the Causes of Saints. If you love bureaucracy, you've come to the right place.

The Vatican is the home of the Catholic religion, but it's also a country. It's a tiny one—only about one hundred acres and less than one thousand residents. The pope is the head of the religion and also the head of Vatican City. Vatican City is old, but its establishment as a territory is a pretty recent development. Its independence was granted in 1929 by Benito Mussolini who was, famously, very much not a saint.

The administration of the Church is run by the Roman Curia, which includes several dicasteries,* or departments, that handle specific

---

* These dicasteries used to be called "congregations." Pope Francis restructured the Roman Curia in 2022 in order to increase transparency and chip away at bureaucratic redundancies. It also means everyone at the Vatican gets new business cards! Good for them!

areas like Catholic education, matters of the clergy, and making saints. These are the folks you'll have to impress if you want to continue up the sainthood ladder. Maybe send a fruit basket.

Every wannabe saint who makes it past Step 2 lands at the Dicastery for the Causes of Saints. The Dicastery was founded in 1588 and was originally called the Sacred Dicastery of Rites, which is much fancier but a lot less clear. They oversee every canonization cause and are in charge of preserving and authenticating relics, which is a later and much spookier step in the canonization process.

By now your cause already has a postulator who, at this point, has moved to Rome to push your cause across the finish line. Think of them like the ultimate mom: they handle all the logistics, get you where you need to go, and talk you up to anyone who will listen. The only difference is that a postulator gets paid for all that work.

All the evidence of your heroic virtues that was gathered by your diocese and sent to Rome is not what will ultimately be presented to the pope. Now your cause gets assigned someone called the "relator." Relators are in charge of working with the postulator to turn all that research into a compelling narrative called a *positio*. *Positio* is Latin for "position," because that's exactly what this is—a long, persuasive essay about your life and why you should be a saint.[†] Seems easy enough, but there is one major wrinkle: It's not enough just to be saint material. You also have to be the type of saint the Church is looking for right now.

In 1983, Pope John Paul II revised and streamlined canonization

---

† Some *positio* are hundreds or even thousands of pages long. They usually get printed multiple times, so you'll also be responsible for sending a lot of trees to heaven.

for the first time in decades, which made sense because (a) the process was horribly outdated and (b) he loved canonizing saints. A lot. During his papacy, John Paul II canonized more than 481 people.[*] He recognized that saints are more than just models of virtue, they are a powerful tool for the Church to communicate what it means to be a good Catholic.

> **WHY ARE SO MANY SAINTS FROM ITALY?**
> The short answer is because so many Catholics are from Italy. The slightly less short answer is this: After Jesus died, his apostles had to flee Jerusalem because of widespread persecution. They wanted to spread the word of God, and the logical place to go was Rome, because of how connected it was to the rest of the world. The phrase "all roads lead to Rome" exists for a reason. Peter (the first pope) was killed in Rome, so that's where his cult of worship began. Rome has been the seat of Catholic religious and political power ever since (with a few schism blips here and there). That means Italian saints basically have home-field advantage.

For example, in 1994, John Paul II beatified now Saint Gianna Molla, an Italian pediatrician who, while pregnant, was diagnosed with a tumor. Gianna refused a lifesaving abortion and instead opted for a dangerous labor. She died of complications shortly after giving birth,

---

[*] So, 482.

but her daughter survived. Selfless? Yes. More selfless than every other saint-to-be waiting in line for beatification? Hard to say. A great example for a Church that just spent decades and millions of dollars pushing for anti-abortion policies across the globe? Absolutely.

Then there's the 2015 canonization of California-based Father Junipero Serra by Pope Francis. Serra has long been a controversial figure because of his efforts to convert Native Americans to Christianity.[†] But Serra was fast-tracked with only one miracle under his belt, seemingly because he presented an opportunity for a fresh pope to canonize someone on American soil[‡] for the first time.

Of course, John Paul II didn't invent the idea of using saints to promote a certain ideal of Catholicism. Canonization has always been used to advance papal agendas. Worried Catholic women are getting a little too sexually liberated? Canonize some virgins! Concerned about the global reach of the Church? Canonize someone on every continent! Struggling with dwindling church attendance from anyone under the age of a Golden Girl? Try Italy's Carlo Acutis. Even though he was just beatified in 2020, Acutis is on the fast track to becoming the first millennial saint and could be canonized as early as 2025. He's already being informally dubbed the patron saint of the internet, which is not a place most people associate with saintly behavior.

The Church has a lot of reasons to want to canonize people, but not a lot of folks to do the job. Ultimately, the Dicastery for the Causes of Saints is a small group of holy guys who meet up twice a month

---

[†] Turns out, they already had their own religion before Serra showed up!
[‡] Originally Native American soil.

and get through around eighty to ninety causes each year. The bottleneck to sainthood is real, so if you want to get that halo, you'd better be holy as hell *and* the pope's type. If you manage to do all those things, you earn a new title: Venerable. But don't celebrate for too long, because the next step is a doozy: it's miracle time.

> **STEP 3: CHECKLIST**
> ✓ Your postulator goes to Rome.
> ✓ You are assigned a relator.
> ✓ Your life story is turned into a *positio*.
> ✓ The big boys in Rome like your *positio*.
> ✓ The pope likes your *positio*, too.
> ✓ You have that "it" factor.

"Money!"*

"The best things in life are free" is a wonderful quote that is not about canonization. Once you become a Servant of God, you need money to support your cause. Halos don't come cheap. Some estimates put the total cost of canonization at around half a million dollars per saint. Exact numbers are hard to pin down, because causes vary greatly in length and scope, and because, historically, the Catholic Church feels the same way about financial matters as it does about predatory priests: they'd rather not discuss it.

---

* Famous prayer from St. Pink Floyd.

Who pays for canonization? Typically, it's the same people who pay for everything else in the Church: regular Catholics. Saints-to-be rely on donations from churches, organizations, and community members to get them over the finish line. It's up to the diocese, along with the postulator (the person who oversees your entire cause from start to finish), to make sure these funds are correctly allocated and tracked. Every cause is like a small business selling the idea of you being in heaven.

Like all small businesses, causes come with a lot of expenses. That postulator needs to get paid. So do the researchers, translators, lawyers, and accountants. Then there are travel expenses, supplies, shipping, printing, office rental, and other administrative costs. That doesn't even include the biggest expense: the canonization mass itself. You'll need programs, chairs, hotels, food, transportation, and of course, a giant banner with your face on it. If you happen to already own a giant banner with your face on it, that would be weird but also a huge help.

This massive expense list is part of why the vast majority of saints are priests, nuns, and popes. Religious orders already have systems in place to solicit and manage donations. For everyone else, it's a steep learning curve. Sainthood has gotten so expensive that even some religious communities now shy away from canonizing their own, finding it hard to justify the cost when they could be doing other things with the money, like feeding the hungry or helping the poor or all the other stuff that one would hope religious communities do with their money.

So, you need to have people supporting your cause who know how to fundraise and manage accounts, have generational money to fall back on, or, in the case of Saint Katharine Drexel, have both. Drexel was a virtuous person who did a lot of good work. She also came from one of the wealthiest families in America. Ever heard of Drexel University? That's them. Katharine made it her life's mission to give away her massive fortune to those in need.* Her sister Louise used some of her money to set up a fund that Katharine's order could use to push her canonization across the finish line. Money won't get you into heaven, but it sure might help people notice you're there.

In an attempt to create more equity among saints, Pope Francis made changes to the financial structure of canonization in 2016. These included demanding more transparency and better accounting on existing causes, as well as the creation of a fund for poor causes.

"I'd love to look at the camera, but I can't really turn my head in this thing." —Katharine

Any cause that makes it to sainthood with leftover cash is expected to put a portion of that money into the fund to support causes from places that aren't financially well-off. It's a great idea that might be working but also might not be, because again, the Vatican doesn't love to talk about money.

If you are less of a "steak and champagne" saint and more of a "ramen and whatever beer was on sale" saint, you should start thinking now about how you're going to pay for your canonization.

---

* No small feat. It's estimated that, in today's currency, her inheritance was around $180 million.

Making a Saint Budget

A halo? In *this* economy?! Sainthood comes with a hefty price tag, so to get ahead of the game, here are some suggestions of ways to fund your one-way ticket to heaven.

1. Create an OnlySaints page. People will pay top dollar for exclusive content of you showing full halo or washing someone's feet with your hair.[†]
2. Make a wedding registry. Why should this just be for people getting married? You deserve an eternity of bliss *and* a Le Creuset casserole dish!
3. Empty your 401(k). If you don't have a 401(k), empty your IRA. If you don't have an IRA, empty your savings. If you don't have savings, start creating that OnlySaints page.
4. Be born to rich parents.
5. Go on *Shark Tank*. To make it seem more like a business, also sell hats or something.
6. Convince an eccentric, elderly widow to leave her fortune to you. Or, if that doesn't work, convince an eccentric, elderly widow to leave her fortune to her French bulldog, then convince the French bulldog to leave his fortune to you.
7. Do one of those things where, if you can spend a whole night in a haunted house, you get to keep the house. Then sell the house to a flipper for cheap. Once it's almost done, ask the ghost to scare the flipper so they sell it back to you

---

[†] It's in the Bible. Google it.

for even cheaper. Then sell the nicely flipped home for top dollar. (Note: you may have to give the ghost a cut.)

8. Sell a kidney. God gave you two for a reason! Okay, technically that reason is to clean your blood and get rid of the waste via urine, but also money! That spare kidney is just a lil' wad of cash, sitting in your lower back.

9. Bake sale!

Don't Beat Yourself Up. Or Maybe Do! Self-Mortification

At this step in the canonization process, folks in Rome will reevaluate your life for evidence that you demonstrated the heroic virtues. Some wannabe saints go above and beyond by practicing something called "self-mortification." Regular mortification is getting your period for the first time while cast as a snowball in the school holiday play.* Self-mortification means enduring pain or self-denial in order to feel closer to God. The idea is that, since Jesus Christ made the ultimate sacrifice for us, performing some form of physical sacrifice brings us closer to him.† Self-mortification is also seen as a way of aggressively rejecting the temptation of sin, unless you think self-harm itself is a sin, in which case, well...okay. Fair point.

---

* Menstruation is normal and nothing to be embarrassed of. However, being cast in a pity part like "snowball" is this sort of scarring experience that can stay with a kid for a lifetime.

† Jesus also did fun stuff like walk on water and turn water into wine, so if you're not into extreme mortification, maybe try emulating Christ by throwing a pool party in wine country!

Attitudes toward self-mortification have changed over history, largely due to the invention of the field of psychology. But it is still done, most recently and notably by Pope John Paul II, who reportedly practiced self-flagellation and sometimes slept on a hard floor. To strike a balance, the Vatican has said that mortification should only be done under the guidance of a spiritual adviser and never for pleasure. So, if you get off on flogging yourself with a whip, you do you, but know that it may hurt your chances of getting a halo.

There are almost unlimited ways to practice self-mortification. Saint Cecilia and Saint Francis of Assisi wore hair shirts: painful undershirts made of either rough cloth or animal hair to irritate the skin. Saint John Vianney practiced severe abstinence of food and sleep. Saint Thomas More practiced self-flagellation.† Mother Teresa used something called a chain cilice—a sharp metal chain wrapped tightly around the thigh. Think of it like medieval torture meets Hot Topic. Mother Teresa also practiced extreme poverty. And every priest, nun, bishop, cardinal, and pope practices celibacy.§

Even at the most basic, nonsaint level, all Catholics are called on to practice some sort of mortification in the form of sacrifice, traditionally during Lent. Lent takes place during the forty days leading up to Easter and is when Catholics are asked to give up meat on Fridays as well as something additional of their own choosing to purify their souls and unite with Christ through suffering. This usually means giving up something

---

† Flogging yourself as a form of self-discipline. The character Silas in *The DaVinci Code* practiced this. And the same actor plays Vision in the Marvel movies. This book contains so much information!

§ Or at least says they will.

like sweets, coffee, alcohol, or, more traditionally, saying you're going to give up one of those things and then caving in on day three.

These baby sacrifices during Lent might be enough for the average Catholic, but you're going to have to amp it up if you want a front-row seat in heaven. However, realistically, full-on medieval style self-mortification is tough and cilices are pricey, so here are some updated forms of self-mortification for the aspiring saint.

OUT: Hairshirt.
IN: Overalls. Even the most fashionable overalls make you look like a giant toddler. Plus, there is no elegant way to use a public bathroom while wearing them. They are flattering on exactly zero percent of the population. Truly a modern form of torture.
OUT: Self-flagellation.
IN: Getting a tattoo that a drunk friend picked out for you. The experience causes physical pain, and the mark left behind is probably something you'll regret.
OUT: Extreme fasting.
IN: Drinking decaf coffee. What is the point?
OUT: Going barefoot in all climates.
IN: Ballet flats. They are somehow more painful than being barefoot.
OUT: Celibacy.
IN: Watching a movie that has a graphic sex scene while your parents are in the room. Truly, this is a suffering the early saints could not have imagined.
OUT: Kneeling for long periods of time.
IN: Being over 30 and having knees. It's the pain of extended kneeling, all the time, for reasons as simple as, "I sat weird yesterday."

OUT: Chain cilice.

IN: Using an old razor to shave. It's an equally effective way to tear your flesh. For a bonus, put on scented lotion after and offer up the vanilla scented burning sensation as a sacrifice to Jesus.

OUT: Vow of poverty.

IN: Being a millennial trying to afford a home.

OUT: Abstaining from sleep.

IN: Having children.

Saints Who Did the Most

For much of Church history, self-mortification was a common practice among Catholics who were concerned about rejecting the temptations of Satan. The idea behind self-mortification is that, by denying the pleasures of Earth, the soul is brought closer to heaven. In practice, that means self-harm, which is why mortification has largely fallen out of favor in the contemporary Church. These days, the practice lives on in small sacrifices like giving up pleasures for Lent, rejecting vices, and subjecting yourself to acoustic guitar renditions of "How Great Thou Art" during the cool weekend mass.

These are a few of the saints who took mortification to the next level. If you run into them in heaven, don't tell them about developments in psychology. It'll just bum them out.

Saint Catherine of Genoa (1447–1510)

Catherine was an intense kid. When she was as young as eight years old, she refused to sleep in her normal bed, opting instead for a bed of straw and a wooden block for a pillow. Against her wishes, her parents married her off at sixteen, which went about as well as you'd expect. As if a bad marriage isn't hard enough, Catherine kept on making life harder. A short list of her preferred self-mortifications includes licking the ground, wearing a hair shirt, refusing to eat meat or fruit, eventually refusing to eat anything at all, and keeping her eyes cast downward. Surprisingly, this lifestyle must've been appealing, because her husband converted and agreed to live a celibate life with her—which one imagines wasn't super hard given the fact that her lingerie was a hair shirt.

Saint Hilarion (c. 291–c. 371)

Hilarion was a hermit who took dietary self-mortification to the next level. Starting around age twenty, he spent three years eating only moistened lentils, then three years eating only dry bread and salt water, then three years only herbs and roots, followed by four years of barley bread and veggies (a treat compared to the previous nine years). Somehow, despite what must've been an insane case of malnutrition and the worst-smelling farts in history, Hilarion survived. At age sixty-four, he stopped eating bread (ahead of his time in terms of diet trends). Oh, and he did much of this while living in a five-foot-by-five-foot cell. Hilarion lived to be eighty years old and is now in heaven hopefully enjoying a whole Costco sheet cake.

Saint Celestine V (c. 1215–1296)

Celestine V was, against his will, a pope. Starting his life as Peter, Celestine V just wanted to be a hermit and live his life in intense devotion to God. This included things like wearing a hair shirt (standard), draping himself with iron chains (advanced), and spending the better part of every year consuming just bread and water (extreme). All these supercool hobbies made Celestine so popular that he attracted enough followers to found his own holy order: the Celestines. Despite his best efforts to be alone, Celestine couldn't fight his popularity and was named pope in 1294.* It was a cool job with a lot of power, and Celestine hated it. Thankfully, due to internal fighting, his papacy didn't last long. Celestine V was pressured to resign just months after taking office and, to prevent any future power struggles, was put in prison until his death two years later. So ultimately, he did get his wish to be left alone!

Saint John Marie Vianney (1786–1859)

John didn't get much formal education as a kid, which caused him to struggle when he entered the seminary. But once John was ordained a priest in 1815, he went hard. He practiced extreme fasting and would work between sixteen and twenty hours a day hearing confession, proving that man can survive on hot goss alone. But that wasn't enough for ole John. He also reportedly slept on a board, wore chains, wouldn't shoo away bugs that landed on him, and refused to smell flowers. Yes, John's dedication to God was so extreme that he literally refused to stop and smell the roses.

---

* Due to a weird scheduling issue, he actually is the only pope in history to have two different papal coronation ceremonies. Must've been torture for a guy who didn't want to be pope in the first place.

Saint Rose of Lima (1586–1617)

Rose of Lima committed to a life of prayer at a young age and never looked back. Concerned that her beauty was a distraction, she rubbed her face with peppers and her hands with quicklime until they were red and blistered. She cut off her hair and wore a spiked crown to mimic Jesus's crown of thorns. She practiced extreme fasting, sometimes refusing even water. She flogged herself regularly, wore a hair shirt, and slept on a bed of broken glass and stone. Oh, and all this was in her twenties. Rose experienced many visions throughout her life, possibly due to the whole constant torture and dehydration thing. Years of severe mortification may be great for the soul but not for the body, and Rose passed away at the relatively young age of thirty-one. She's typically depicted in art wearing a crown of roses and looking absolutely radiant, which must annoy the shit out of her.

"Crap, I look spectacular, don't I?" —Rose

Saints Who Did the Bare Minimum

If whipping yourself and wearing spiked chains around your thighs sounds like a lot, don't worry. The history of sainthood is full of people who did extraordinary things, overcame unbelievable odds, made unthinkable sacrifices, and contributed to the advancement of not just Catholicism, but also all human history. Then there's these guys.

You know these guys. You've gone to school with them. You've worked with them. You may have even dated them. They're the ones who keep getting promoted despite not knowing how to attach a PDF to an email. The ones who are thirty-five yet somehow don't know how to use a breaker box. The dads who call taking care of their own children "babysitting." These guys are everywhere, even heaven.

Saint Adrian III (d. c. 885)

Historians don't know much about who Adrian III was or why he got the big halo promotion. He was elected pope in 884, which means he only reigned for about a year before he died. During that time, his major accomplishments seem to have been sentencing one member of an opposition party to blinding and then death and having a woman who was a part of that same opposition party whipped and paraded through the streets naked. Adrian III died on his way to visit the unfortunately named King Charles III the Fat. He wasn't martyred; he just didn't survive the trip. Now, for reasons that remain unclear, he's a saint.

Saint Anastasius I (d. 401)

Anastasius I was only pope for about two years. His most notable contribution to church history seems to be that he was the first pope to say that priests should stand up and bow their heads while reading the Gospel.* It's a nice gesture, but maybe not halo-worthy. It's sort of like putting your dishes in the sink after Thanksgiving dinner and

---

* And maybe being Innocent I's daddy. (See "Saints Who Were Nepo Babies.")

wanting as much credit as the person who got up at 5:00 a.m. to cook the turkey. We're all proud of you for helping, but like, calm down.

Saint Hyginus (d. c. 140)

Hyginus was the ninth pope, and that's about all we know about him. The heretical belief of Gnosticism seemed to gain ground during his papacy, but there's no record of him doing anything about it. Nobody knows how Hyginus died, but he isn't listed on any martyrologies, so it seems like natural causes. Basically, the only three known facts about him are (1) he was briefly pope, (2) he eventually died, and (3) he's a saint.

Saint Fabian (d. 250)

Fabian was a martyr and pope who actually made several important contributions to the Church during his reign, including organizing the role of deacons in Rome and making infrastructure improvements to the catacombs of Saint Callistus. It's how he became pope that earns him a spot on this list. Fabian was a farmer who just happened to visit Rome when a new pope was being elected. A dove landed on Fabian, which the electors took as a sign, so they unanimously voted for him to be the next pope. That's it. His

"Aww, I'm pretty sure I just invented finger guns, but nobody cares cuz real guns haven't been invented yet." —Fabian

whole resume was "man with bird on him." The lesson here is, the next time you have a job interview and feel underqualified, just fill your pockets with birdseed and hope you can pull a Fabian.

Saint James the Greater (d. 44)

James was one of the Twelve Apostles and, after Jesus was killed, likely went on to travel and preach. Not much is known about James's post-Jesus life, and it may have been amazing, but that's not why he got the nickname "the Greater." James gets to carry that honorable distinction for the rest of his afterlife for the sole reason that he was taller than another apostle who was also named James. Even worse, the shorter guy got stuck with the nickname James the Lesser, which just feels mean.

Saints Who Didn't Get Out Much

If you don't want to be a martyr, a pope, or eat nothing but bread for the rest of your life, you still have another option for standing out from the holy crowd: become a hermit. In Catholicism, hermits are people who opt to live a life of solitude, prayer, and minimal comforts. If your ideal vacation is wandering alone in the desert for decades, hermit life might be for you!

Hermits practice something called asceticism, which is the practice of extreme repression and self-denial. The idea is that to free yourself from mortal failings, you must first overcome bodily temptations. Asceticism is not a term exclusive to Catholics. Most religions have some form of ascetic practice in their history. The idea has even bled into secular life. If you've ever Marie Kondo'd your home in the hopes of living a more peaceful, centered life, you've technically practiced a mini version of asceticism. Also, you probably bought a ton of storage boxes and annoyed your friends by going on and on about which sweaters brought you joy.

When widespread persecution of Christians by the Romans started to decline in the fourth century, the faithful had to look for other ways to emulate Christ. With fewer opportunities to suffer like Christ in death, the hot new craze became suffering like him in life. Enter hermits. Hermits would reject every worldly comfort from society to clothing, even food. Their lives were devoted totally to prayer (and the occasional good deed or preaching gig) and achieving a sort of religious euphoria through bodily suffering. You know how marathoners talk about a "runner's high"? It's like that, only hermits didn't get fun medals and foil blankets when they were done.

> **MONKS**
>
> A monk is someone who decides to live their life in an insular community (like a monastery), away from the trappings of society. Monks lead a contemplative life, meaning they spend their days mostly alone in thought and prayer, meditating on God. It's like a retreat, but forever and with no spa services.

People tend to think of old men when they think of hermits, but many of the earliest Catholic hermits were women. In fact, the word "nun" is a derivative of the Latin *nonnus*, which is the feminine of "monk." Very few stories of the female hermits remain because history was usually written by guys, and guys sure do love writing about other guys. Also, there are very few first-person accounts of what hermit life was like because being alone was kind of the whole hermit deal.

If you crave the life of a hermit but give off more of an "indoor cat" vibe, you might want to consider another solitary option: anchorite. While hermits tended to live out their lives exposed to the elements, anchorites lived (and eventually died) sealed into what could generously be described as walk-in closets (that you don't walk out of). When anchorites decided to devote their lives to prayer, they were taken in by a church, which constructed a small room "anchored" to a wall of the building. The anchorite would be sealed inside with only small windows through which food and chamber pots could be passed (and hopefully not mixed up) and the altar inside the church could be seen. Think of it like a sensory deprivation tank, but forever.

Anchorites, who were typically women, sacrificed physical connection to the world in order to focus entirely on prayer. And when they died, they were often buried in the room where they lived, which must've been extra creepy for the next anchorite on deck to move in. The anchorite lifestyle never caught on in the same way the hermit lifestyle did because (a) it cost money and (b) wow, it sounds really unpleasant.

Meanwhile, the big struggle for hermits was that they became super popular. Many would preach about their experiences, which amassed followers and drew others into the hermit life. Things got a little touchy with the clergy since hermits, by definition, existed outside of Church structure. Plus, for a young religion looking to attract new followers, hermits set kind of a high bar. If the choice was between convert to Christianity and live alone in a loincloth in the desert forever until you die or just stay comfortably pagan, understandably a lot of people would go with the pagan option.

Today, the legacy of those early hermits and anchorites is seen in monks. Monks live ascetic lives, typically in communities with other monks. They also often serve their larger community in some way by doing things like teaching or volunteering. Monastic life is perfect for anyone who wants the deprivation of being a hermit but also the freedom to wander around Target once in a while.

There are lots of different ways to live your best hermit life. Here are some of Catholicism's most famous examples to guide you.

Saint Anthony (251–356)

Anthony is credited with being the OG Catholic monk. When Anthony was a young man, his parents died, leaving him in charge of the family estate. Desiring a religious life, Anthony sold the land and possessions, plopped his sister in a nunnery,* and disappeared into the desert for a few decades. When he finally reemerged in his fifties, he founded a monastery where he could teach others all that he learned during his years alone with God. After spending decades eating nothing but old bread, salt, and water, Anthony is said to have lived to the ripe old age of 105. So, yes, every diet is bullshit.

---

* No word on whether that's where his sister wanted to be plopped.

Saint Benedict (c. 480–c. 547)

Anthony might be the first monk, but Benedict is the one who put monks on the map. Benedict only lived as a hermit for about three years starting at the age of fourteen.[†] The solo life wasn't a great fit for him, so he founded his own monastery and wrote something called the Rule: his regulations for how to live like a monk. Because early hermits kind of made things up as they went along, there was a ton of variety in what ascetic life looked like. Benedict's Rule finally codified what it means to be a Catholic ascetic. It called for obedience, prayer, and work for your community. The union of solitary prayer plus community work proved to be a winning combo, and Benedictines are now one of the largest religious orders in the world. Benedict also had to leave his hermit career because he had an active side job as a miracle worker. Just a few of the miracles attributed to him include curing the sick, raising the dead, multiplying food, enabling someone to walk on water, prophesizing, predicting his own death, and manifesting money. Kind of a waste to make money out of thin air if you're living alone in the desert.

Saint Simeon (390–459)

Hermits can technically live wherever they want as long as they have solitude. Saint Anthony of Egypt spent his days in abandoned ruins in the desert, Saint Mary of Egypt lived wandering outside, and then there's Saint Simeon the Stylite, who lived on a three-foot-wide pillar fifty feet in the air.

[†] This means Benedict spent his formative teen years alone in the desert, which is honestly not a bad idea.

"Life on the pole isn't all it's cracked up to be." —Simeon

Simeon was drawn to religious life at a young age. He joined a monastery but was asked to leave for being a bit extra. He tried his hand at normal hermit life—fasting, practicing celibacy, living in a meager hut—but that still wasn't enough for Simeon. So, he took the next logical step: he built a platform on top of a nine-foot pillar[*] and lived up there.

For some reason, this attracted a lot of attention. People constantly interrupted Simeon's prayers with questions like "what?" and "why?" and "um...what?" Undeterred, Simeon had a flawless solution: taller pillar! He upped the height to fifty to sixty feet[†] and lived up there for the last thirty-seven years of his life.

Lest living on a pole four stories in the air become too cozy, Simeon continually sought out new ways to take asceticism to the extreme. Legend says he ate only one meal a week, stood for long stretches on one leg, practiced self-mortification, and then requested that maggots be brought to him so he could place them in his wounds. He was the Johnny Knoxville of saints.

---

[*] Some sources say his first pillar was only six feet, but at a certain point, once you're living on a pillar, the height isn't really the big issue.

[†] Again, nobody knows the exact height, but since he's a guy, we have to assume he rounded up by at least a few inches.

If all of this sounds too insane to believe, buckle up, because the actual most insane part of the story is that Simeon was so incredibly popular that A WHOLE BUNCH OF OTHER PEOPLE STARTED LIVING ON PILLARS. After shifting to a taller pillar, Simeon drew even bigger crowds (shocking), and he would shout his teachings down to the pilgrims below. Inspired by Simeon's devotion to God, they decided to follow his teachings and call themselves stylites. There were enough of them that "stylite" is today generally considered a subcategory of hermits.

So, if you think you have what it takes to live a life of extreme deprivation and you don't have a fear of heights, the stylite life might be for you. Also, to answer your question, he would lower down a poop bucket to his disciples.‡

STEP 3 COMPLETE!
Achievement Unlocked: Venerable
THE PROS:
- You have your second official title. Time to print new heavenly business cards.

THE CONS:
- Lots of people get stuck at Venerable because miracles are pretty hard to do.
- "Venerable" is higher up than "Servant of God" but sounds less badass.

---

‡ Don't act like that wasn't what you were wondering this whole time.

PATRON SAINTS
Finding Your Thing

ave you ever heard anyone say, "I'm praying to Saint Jude"* about you? If so, they were talking about patron saints. Patron saints spend eternity looking out for specific places, professions, or causes. Basically, if God is the CEO, patron saints are the department managers.

Patron saints intervene on behalf of humans with God. So, if you have a big test coming up, you might pray to Saint Ursula, the patron saint of students. Got appendicitis? Pray to Saint Elmo. (Also go to the hospital.) Want to work in a lighthouse? Try Saint Verena, patron saint of lighthouse keepers. Live in Dubuque, Iowa? That's too bad. Try praying to Saint John Vianney, patron saint of Dubuque. You get the idea.

All of these saints are patrons of things they had a special connection to in life. For example, before becoming an apostle, Saint Matthew was a tax collector, which is why he's now the patron saint of

---

* St. Jude is the patron saint of impossible causes. If anyone ever said this to you, it was an insult. Sorry.

accountants. Saint Joan of Arc briefly led the French army and is now the patron saint of France. Why is Saint Elmo the patron of abdominal pain? Because he was disemboweled. Not exactly a tummy ache, but for Catholics, close enough!

The trick here is to become a patron saint of something that people really care about. Saint Christopher has remained popular despite being fictional in part because he's the patron saint of traveling, which, it turns out, people do every day. Meanwhile, Saint Gummarus was probably great, but not many people are calling on the patron saint of lumberjacks anymore. In addition to things like occupations and locations, Catholics also occasionally celebrate "name days," or the feast day of the saint with whom they share a name. Again, things aren't looking good for Saint Gummarus.

Most saints are patrons of something, and many are patrons of multiple things, so if you want to stand out from the crowd, you'll have to find a hook that makes you unique. The good news is there are plenty of occupations, causes, and places still in need of a patron. Here's a very brief list of what's taken and what's still on the table![†]

- **ACTORS:** Saints Genesius and Vitus
- **ACTRESSES:** Saint Pelagia
- **THAT THING WHERE THEY SAY "NEW YORK CITY IS REALLY ONE OF THE CHARACTERS":** still available!
- **AIR TRAVELERS:** Saint Joseph of Cupertino

[†] There's currently no patron saint of writing lists. It could be you! Start by writing a list of reasons why you'd be a great fit for that job.

- **AIR TRAVELERS WHO GET STUCK WITH THE MIDDLE SEAT:** still available!
- **ARTISTS:** Saint Luke the Evangelist
- **EXPLAINING TO YOUR PARENTS THAT ART SCHOOL IS REAL SCHOOL:** still available!
- **BREASTFEEDING:** Saint Giles
- **SWITCHING TO FORMULA BECAUSE OF CRACKED NIPPLES:** still available!
- **BROKEN BONES:** Saint Stanislaus Kostka
- **WHEN YOU STUB YOUR TOE AND AREN'T SURE IF IT'S BROKEN, SO YOU JUST TAPE IT TO THE BUDDY TOE BECAUSE THAT'S ALL THE DOCTOR WOULD DO ANYWAY:** still available!
- **CHICKEN FARMERS:** Saint Brigid
- **COFFEEHOUSE KEEPERS:** Saint Drogo
- **KNOWING THE STARBUCKS BATHROOM CODE:** still available!
- **CORN CHANDLERS:** Saint Honoratus of Amiens
- **KNOWING WHAT A CORN CHANDLER IS:** still available!
- **DROUGHT (AGAINST):** Saint Godeberta
- **DROUGHT (FOR):** still available!
- **EUROPE:** Saint Benedict
- **LISTENING TO SOMEONE WHO DEFINITELY DIDN'T PAY THEIR OWN COLLEGE TUITION TALK ABOUT HOW THEY TOOK A GAP YEAR TO BACKPACK ACROSS EUROPE AND "ROUGH IT":** still available!
- **FAMILIES:** Saint Joseph

- **FAMILY HARMONY:** Saint Dymphna
- **COWORKERS WHO SAY, "YOU'RE MY WORK FAMILY!" (AGAINST):** still available!
- **HAIRSTYLISTS:** Saints Martin de Porres and Mary Magdalene
- **BANGS:** still available!
- **LAUNDRESSES:** Saint Clare of Assisi, Hunna, and Veronica
- **TELLING SOMEONE TO DO THEIR OWN DAMN LAUNDRY:** still available!
- **MESSENGERS:** Gabriel the Archangel
- **AOL INSTANT MESSENGER:** still available!
- **SEAFOOD:** Saint Corentin
- **CHICKEN OF THE SEA FOOD:** still available!
- **TEACHERS:** Saints Catherine of Alexandria, Francis de Sales, John Baptist de la Salle, and Gregory I
- **PAYING TEACHERS MORE AND/OR AT LEAST NOT MAKING THEM BUY THEIR OWN SUPPLIES:** still available!

CAN MY DOG BE A SAINT?

umans have always had a lot of questions about heaven. Will I see my family again? Will I be my sick, old self or my hot, younger self? Can I bring my dog? The answer to the first two is: who the hell knows. But the latter has been given some attention and even some hazy answers. Here's what a few recent popes have had to say on the matter:

"Paradise is open to all of God's creatures."—Pope Paul VI

"Holy Scripture teaches us that the fulfillment of this wonderful design also affects everything around us, and that came out of the thought and the heart of God."—Pope Francis

"For other creatures, who are not called to eternity, death just means the end of existence on Earth."—Pope Benedict XVI

"Eww! Spider!"—Some pope at some point, probably

It's understandable that people want animals to go to heaven. Animals are great. We love them. In fact, we love animals so much that, in 2022, Pope Francis gave a speech criticizing people who chose to have pets over children, implying they are selfish. Kind of harsh coming from a guy who doesn't have kids and calls his followers his "flock."

But if animals do go to heaven, that raises some logistic issues. Having pets is one thing, but most animals on the planet aren't available for adoption at Petco. Every extinct animal would be in heaven. So would every fish and whale. Where would they swim? Or can they fly in heaven? Would they even like that? Also, they'd be right up there with the fishermen and whalers who killed them. Awkward.

If all animals have souls, then every rat would also be in heaven. Even worse, every bug. Think of how long bugs live. Now think about every bug that ever lived, ever, being in heaven. Spending eternity with every spider in the history of spiders sure sounds more like hell than paradise. And what about plants? They are technically alive. Also, a large number of plants are dead because we killed them,* so that really makes it seem like they deserve eternal paradise.

On the plus side, since every extinct animal would be in heaven, that means dinosaurs are there, too. It would be like good Jurassic Park. A *T. rex* is already cool, now imagine a *T. rex* with a halo. It almost makes up for spending eternity with eight bajillion mosquitos.

If the logic is that everything with a soul can go to heaven, then

---

* Apologies to the tree who died for this book! Hope you're in heaven hanging out with some cool shrubs!

can animals also go to hell? Heaven having an open-door policy to all animals seems unfair. They can't get baptized or conceptualize virtues like faith, hope, and charity. On the other hand, imagine dying and finding out your childhood dog went to hell. Seems mean. But dogs also can't repent or do penance. And anyone who's had a dog who got into the trash and ate a bunch of hair and then pooped out the hair but it got stuck so you had to stand on the street and pull hair poop out of your dog's butt* knows, they are not without sin.

Maybe someday the Vatican will issue a definitive statement on whether or not animals can enter the Pearly Gates. Until then, just know that praying for your beloved puppy to go to heaven also means spending eternity with every millipede ever.

---

*   A very common thing that has happened to everyone, obviously.

SAINTS WHO WERE VERY GOOD BOYS

Saint Guinefort was brave, selfless, and probably licked his balls, because Saint Guinefort was a dog.

This is how the legend goes: back in the thirteenth century, a knight and his wife left their castle for some reason. Maybe a night on the town, maybe hunting, we don't know for sure because again, this is a legend. Anyway, they left their baby in the care of their faithful greyhound, Guinefort. When they returned home, the baby was missing and the dog was covered in blood. The knight leapt to the conclusion that the dog killed the baby and immediately ran him through with his sword. Sounds impulsive, but we're also talking about a parent who left his infant in the care of a dog, so maybe he wasn't great at making decisions.

Unfortunately, this knight wasn't just a negligent dad, he was also totally wrong. Moments later he and his wife found their baby, alive and well, hiding in a corner. Near the baby was a dead serpent. Turns out, the blood on Guinefort wasn't from their child, it was from the serpent, which he had killed to protect the baby. Turns out Guinefort was a great babysitter.

The story could've ended there, but soon after, the knight's castle fell to ruin, which the locals believed was God seeking vengeance for the unjust murder of such a very good boy. They did the only logical thing medieval peasants could do and started venerating the dog as a martyr and saint.[*]

The Church was understandably not a fan of making a dog into a saint. For one thing, popes have been murky on whether or not animals can even go to heaven. As recently as 2014, Pope Francis implied that animals could earn a spot in heaven, but it's not official doctrine. Religious officials at the time dismissed any miracles attributed to Guinefort as the work of the Devil. The Church tried to suppress the cult of worship surrounding Saint Guinefort and, at one point, there was even a fine imposed on anyone caught worshiping at his shrine (yes, he had a shrine). To this day, Guinefort is not considered an official saint.

Unfortunately for church leaders, Guinefort achieved popular sainthood back when canonization could still be a local, spontaneous affair. While we don't know if dogs go to heaven, it seems pretty clear that people want them there. Because, despite all the Church's efforts, the story of Saint Guinefort has persisted for two main reasons: saints are ultimately products of popular veneration and people really, really love dogs.

---

[*] This isn't an insult. Christianity was still very much figuring itself out in the thirteenth century, so dog saints didn't sound crazier than anything else! It's what scientists call an Air Bud loophole.

STEP 4
Do a Miracle

You're on the homestretch of sainthood! Now all you have to do is perform some miracles. Easy! Right? No. Obviously not. Because these miracles must be complete (meaning not reversed years later), occur after the saint's death, and, in a level of irony that is deeply Catholic, must be investigated and confirmed by a scientific tribunal.

The reason miracles are even required for sainthood is because they're considered the best "evidence" that someone is in heaven. You need two forms of identification to prove heavenly citizenship: either two miracles or martyrdom and one miracle. Basically, canonization operates on passport rules.

The only way to waive that first miracle requirement is to be martyred. One miracle (or being martyred) advances you to the level of beatification where you get the new title of Blessed. But to make it from beatified to canonized, all wannabe saints, martyrs included, must perform that second miracle.

An important technicality is that these must be posthumous miracles. Like Jesus, plenty of saints performed miracles while alive.

It doesn't matter how much you Criss Angel Mindfreaked your way through life. Once you're pushing up daisies, the slate is wiped clean.

The logic is that, while a person is alive, no matter how good they seem, the jury is still out on whether they'll go to heaven. Plus, there's always a possibility that miracles done by someone alive could really be due to intervention from the Devil. Once someone is dead, miracles done in their name must be from God, unless the Devil was doing some sort of trick, which he famously never does.

Lots of things could be considered miraculous: a newborn baby's first laugh, true love, Jim Carrey's transition from physical comedy to leading dramatic roles.* But in the eyes of the Church, the most likely miracles to get approved by the Vatican—and therefore the type most often presented for consideration—are medical miracles. We're talking healings, cures, restoration of lost abilities (sight, hearing, movement, etc.), basically anything that would make a great episode of *House*.

All miracles up for consideration get investigated by a team of doctors in Rome called the Consulta Medica. Established in the mid-1900s, the Consulta Medica consists of about a hundred doctors, and each miracle is assigned a team of five. That team is responsible for reviewing every medical file, scan, X-ray, and sometimes the actual patient in order to study the alleged miracle. The doctors are paid for their work, but not much. Luckily, they also have to be Catholic, so they're unlikely to complain to the pope for a better paycheck.

Each team of doctors studies a miracle and votes on whether the patient's cure is inexplicable. The Consulta Medica doesn't technically

---

* If you didn't tear up at *The Truman Show*, that's a sin.

rule on whether something is a miracle or not—that's up to the theologians. They just determine whether science can explain the outcome. Now, you might ask yourself, "Isn't it possible that results that seem scientifically inexplicable now are just things we haven't figured out yet?" The answer to that question is (a) yes and (b) probably don't ask that if you want to become a saint.

If a supermajority of the doctors rule that the outcome was inexplicable, Vatican theologians then get to work trying to figure out if the results are due to a specific saint's intercession. This is the tricky part, because if a sick person prayed to you and then was cured, perfect! Miracle confirmed! But, if that sick person played the field and prayed to a bunch of saints, there's no way for us dum-dums on Earth to know which saint is ultimately responsible for the miracle. The case is voided and it's back to the heavenly drawing board. So make sure whomever you work your miracles on is monogamous, or you could lose your spot in heaven's line.

The good news is, like all aspects of canonization, the rules are subject to change. In 1980, Pope John II beatified now Saint Kateri Tekakwitha despite the fact that she had no proven miracles, deeming it sufficient that she had a *reputation* for miracles. Pope Francis did something similar in 2014 when he canonized Pope John XXIII with only one confirmed miracle. Meanwhile, Saint Anthony is responsible for so many miracles that he's actually the patron saint of miracles.[†] Show-off.

[†] Some of Anthony's miracles include reviving a boy who drowned when his boat capsized, reviving a boy who fell into a pot of boiling water, reviving a girl who drowned in a pond, and reattaching a severed foot. Thankfully, the foot had not drowned.

Unfortunately, most wannabe saints don't get to skirt the rules. Plus, only about half of all submitted miracles get approval from the Consulta Medica. It's an uphill road, but once you've completed the step of doing two miracles (or one miracle for martyrs), you've made it. Crack open the champagne and break out the fancy crackers,* because you are now just one splashy ceremony away from being a saint!

> **STEP 4: CHECKLIST**
> ✓ Do a miracle.
> ✓ Do another (if needed).

We Should Probably Pause Here to Mention That Some Saints Could Fly

As previously mentioned, the most common types of miracles accepted by the big boys over at the Vatican are posthumous medical miracles. But those aren't the only ones out there. In the past, many saints became famous for performing miracles while alive, which is how we ended up with flying saints.

A person who has such an intimate relationship with God that they gain almost superhuman abilities is called a mystic. These abilities can range from visions (pretty common, sort of cool) to flying (not common, very cool). There used to be a lot of mystics in Catholicism,

---

* Get yourself a wedge of cheese-counter cheese and some of those crackers that cost like six bucks for one sleeve! You've earned it!

but they've become rarer since the invention of cameras and the field of psychology. Weird.

Being a mystic seems like it should be a plus for aspiring saints. It certainly helps with notoriety, and it's hard to argue against your holiness when God is appearing to you in visions and helping you zip around the rooftops like Iron Man.[†] But nowadays, being a mystic is almost a detriment. The contemporary Vatican is understandably wary of people who claim to have God-given superpowers because (a) it's very hard to prove the gifts are from God and not a trick from the Devil and (b) science.

But, while mystic abilities may not be big with the Vatican, they are still very popular with the average Catholic. After all, everyone wants a saint with a good story. So, if you're considering going the mystic route, these are some of your options:

Visions: Skill Level 1. Provability Level 0.

Visions happen when Jesus or Mary or God or another saint appears to you, often in a dream, and gives you either instructions or information. This is good for the mystic starter pack because there's almost no way to prove if you're faking!

Prophecies: Skill Level 3. Provability Level 3.

Prophecies are a little tougher to pull off than visions because it's easy to find out if you're right or wrong. But, if you make enough

---

[†] Okay, technically Iron Man can't fly; the suit can, which means only the suit goes to heaven.

prophecies and keep them vague, odds are you will eventually be correct. That's called meteorology.

> **ODOR OF SANCTITY**
>
> A sweet smell coming off the body of some incorrupt saints. It also sometimes comes off a saint's garments or surrounds them while they're still alive. Usually described as sweet or floral, which is nice considering how bad humans smelled for most of history.

Incorruptibility: Skill Level 6. Provability Level 5.

It's debatable whether this is technically a mystic power, because it happens after the saint is dead. Incorruptibility is when the dead body of a saint is exhumed and found to show no signs of decay and/or gives off the odor of sanctity. This is usually taken as a sign of the person's holiness and of the fact that, for most of human history, we didn't fully understand how temperature, moisture, and soil content impacted decomposition.*

---

* The existence of the sweet odor of sanctity means there are people out there who need to sniff dead bodies to see if they might be saints. Just a fun thing to think about as you try to fall asleep tonight!

Bilocation: Skill Level 7. Provability Level 7.

Bilocation is the ability to be in two places at once. Every mom has the mystical power of bilocation.

Inedia: Skill Level 9. Provability Level 8.

Inedia is Latin for "not eating," which is exactly what it is. Mystics with inedia can survive for months or even years on little to no food. Often the only food that sustains them is the Eucharist, a.k.a. the body of Christ. Unfortunately for mystics with inedia, the body of Christ is usually presented as a tiny little cracker and not an entire Thanksgiving turkey.

Stigmata: Skill Level 10. Provability Level 9.

The stigmata are the wounds of Christ on the cross, which usually means some combination of nail wounds on the hands and feet, marks on the head from the crown of thorns, and a spear wound in the side. Someone with stigmata is considered to be as close to Christ as you can get since they are literally experiencing his suffering. Stigmata is incredibly rare and absolutely ruins your bedsheets.

Levitation/Flying: Skill Level 10. Provability Level 10.

Levitation and flying are pretty self-explanatory. This one gets a slightly higher provability level than stigmata because, while you can theoretically fake wounds, it's pretty hard to fake flying. While this power is less overtly Christlike than the stigmata, it does sound way more fun.

Saints Who Could Do Cool Shit

Being a mystic is very cool, and Catholic history is full of saints with mystic abilities. So if you are thinking of going down this road, you should get to know a few of your heavenly buds.

Saint Hildegard of Bingen (1098–1179)

Mystic abilities: visions

Aside from having a great name, Hildegard of Bingen was a prominent Catholic mystic and feminist. She started having visions as a child and was sent to a cloister (like a convent but more shut off from the world) when she was eight years old. In her visions, God encouraged little Hildie to write, and boy did she. Over her life, she cranked out books on religion and medicine; composed seventy-seven songs, a musical morality play, fifty homilies, and three hundred letters. She also invented her own language complete with an alphabet. Oh, and she didn't even start work on any of this until after the age of forty, which, in the twelfth century, meant she was a senior citizen.

"It's my latest idea. I call it the Squatty Potty." —Hildegard

Women during Hildegard's time weren't usually permitted to read or write, let alone become more prolific than Stephen King. But Ms. Bingen found a loophole: this successful career wasn't her idea—it was God's! Over the course of her life, God also told her that she should stand up to the pope and other high-ranking clergy, that men and women should be equals, and that sex is fun and shouldn't just be for procreation. Again, not her opinion—all God's!

Saint Francis of Assisi (c. 1181–1226)

Mystic abilities: visions, stigmata, talking to animals, controlling the weather, multiplying food

Saint Francis of Assisi is famous for having the first verified case of stigmata, but that is far from his only claim to fame. After a wild and crazy youth, God came to Francis in a series of visions and told him to get his shit together and live a life of service. Francis did exactly that, selling some of his father's expensive cloth to pay to rebuild a local church.

It was a sweet gesture, but Francis probably should've asked for his dad's permission first. Due to his unauthorized cloth sale, Francis was shunned by his family. He got

"Look, I keep telling you, we can't thumb wrestle because you have no thumbs." —Francis

himself a dozen followers and convinced them all to join him in a life of poverty, working with the needy, and shaving just the tops of their heads (which seems like a harder sell than the life of poverty part).

In addition to visions and stigmata, Francis had the gifts of multiplying food, controlling the weather, and talking to animals who, legend says, would gather to listen to him preach. In one famous story, he visited a town that was being terrorized by a wolf and told the people that, if they fed the wolf every day, the attacks would stop. They did. Instead of attacking, the wolf just went door to door every day, begging for food. So, Francis is either a miracle worker or the first person to domesticate a dog.

"Look ma! No photographic evidence!" —Joseph

Saint Joseph of Cupertino (1603–1663)

Mystic abilities: visions, flying, levitation, bilocation, prophecy, inedia

Joseph of Cupertino had a ton of mystic powers but was most famous for his ability to fly. So much so that he earned himself a nickname: The Flying Friar. Joseph's flights would happen as a result of religious ecstasy, which happened pretty much anytime he thought about God. Pretty inconvenient considering he was a friar and thinking about God is kind of their whole deal. His flying became such a disruptive spectacle that he was eventually forbidden from saying mass and participating in regular activities with his fellow friars. Hard to believe that stopped him, given that he allegedly also had the ability to bilocate.

The haters didn't slow Joseph down (or keep him grounded). Over the course of his life, he flew dozens of times and even once carried a fellow friar around the room, which is admirable. It seems like, if you have the ability to fly, the least you could do is give your friends rides every once in a while.

In addition to flying and bilocating, Joseph practiced inedia. He is said to have eaten solid foods only twice a week for thirty-five years. He also had visions and prophecies, which in hindsight were probably related to the whole "always being on the brink of starvation" thing.

Saint Padre Pio (1887–1968)

Mystic abilities: you name it

Padre Pio was a controversial figure during his life because he wasn't just any mystic, he was THE mystic. He could do it all: visions, prophecies, stigmata, bilocation, healings, miracles—even the blood coming from his stigmata wounds reportedly smelled like flowers. He was like a magician crossed with a Glade PlugIn.

Stigmata is a relatively rare ability, but not for Padre Pio. He received the wounds of Christ on and off for the last fifty years of his life. It was such a common occurrence that he had to wear specially designed gloves and shoes to keep the wounds covered. Sounds like a major inconvenience but, upon receiving the stigmata for the first time, his tuberculosis went away, so you win some, you lose some.

Chronic stigmata didn't slow down Padre Pio. Thanks to his gift of bilocation, he traveled the world performing healings and responding to prayers. So really his ultimate miracle was never once having to wait in line at the airport.

Padre Pio's popularity was his gift and his curse. For a long time, the Church tried to keep him quiet. In 1923, he was ordered to stop writing letters and publicly preaching. Remember, the Church wants the public to honor saints but not worship them. Due to his boatload of abilities, Padre Pio ran the danger of being venerated not *because* of God, but *as* a God. His popularity eventually won out, and Padre Pio was canonized in 2002. He remains incredibly popular, which makes sense since he could literally do it all.

Saint Gemma Galgani (1878–1903)

Mystic abilities: visions, stigmata, levitation, could smell evil, used her guardian angel like a mailman

Saint Gemma did not have an easy life. She was chronically ill, her mother passed away when she was a child, and she eventually came down with a bad case of meningitis. As if all of that wasn't enough, at the age of twenty-one she experienced the stigmata. And kept experiencing it. She continued to show the stigmata every weekend for two years, which really must've made it impossible to plan a vacation.

On top of her regular Friday night stigmata, Gemma also had an extremely active visionary life. She had frequent battles with the Devil and had a buddy-buddy relationship with her guardian angel. They would talk for hours, get into spats, and—in a move that seems super beneath the job of angel—he would carry messages for her. If she had something to tell someone, instead of sending a letter, she would tell her guardian angel to deliver the message for her and bring back a response. People confirmed they got the messages, so it seems like Gemma's true mystic ability is that she invented email.

Unclaimed Miracles

The vast majority of miracles accepted by the Dicastery for the Causes of Saints are medical miracles, like curing diseases or healing injuries. If you really want to stand out from the crowd, here are some deeply important yet often overlooked medical miracles that are still up for grabs:

1. Curing someone who has that annoying thing where you're congested but only one nostril is plugged up and the other one somehow breathes too well.
2. Granting someone a miraculous body that fits perfectly into bridesmaid dresses every time with zero alterations.
3. Curing the pain that results from being kicked in the balls while somehow retaining how funny it is to see someone get kicked in the balls.
4. Giving someone the gift of boobs that stay the same size their entire lives so they don't have to keep spending money on new bras.
5. Blessing two partners with the miracle of both craving the same thing for dinner at the same time, all the time.
6. Giving someone the miracle of a period that never coincides with vacation.

7. Blessing someone with the ability to, for their entire lives, sleep through the whole night without ever having to get up to pee.
8. Curing someone who has that thing where cilantro tastes like soap.
9. Blessing all parents with the ability to nurse in public without weirdos being weirdos about it.
10. Curing someone's pet allergies, unless it's an allergy to a pet belonging to someone whose house they want to leave, in which case the miracle would be to make that allergy way worse.
11. Blessing someone with the ability to look great in every style of jeans.
12. Granting someone the ability to fall asleep without spending an hour lying in bed, staring at the ceiling, and mentally cataloging every interaction they had that day based on how awkward they think they were.
13. Allowing a guy to know everything about *Star Wars* and yet somehow resist the urge to explain it to anyone else.
14. Granting someone a miraculous face that can actually pull off a soul patch.
15. Curing someone who feels compelled to always say, "Well this is going straight to my hips!" after consuming any form of food that contains calories.
16. Curing someone who is in that in-between phase of growing out a pixie cut.
17. You know that thing where your eye starts twitching and it

doesn't hurt but it just drives you nuts because it's all you can focus on? Yeah, cure that.

18. End all hiccups. Or, at the very least, bless humanity with one universal, effective cure for hiccups so we can all stop wasting our time scouring the internet for tricks like "hold your nose and drink water" or "hang upside down and sing 'Happy Birthday' ten times."
19. Cure all cancer. For everybody. Everywhere. Because wouldn't it be baller to be the saint who did a nice thing just because, instead of doling out miracles one at a time, only to people who ask you directly? Worth a shot!
20. If curing all cancer is too big of an ask, maybe cure all papercuts. Not cancer, but still helpful!

STEP 4 COMPLETE!
Achievement Unlocked: Blessed
THE PROS:
- You've been beatified, which earns you the penultimate title of Blessed.
- You can now be venerated at the local level. International fame is for saints only.
- You can now be painted with a version of a halo that looks like rays shooting out from behind your head. Think of it like the training bra of halos.

THE CONS:
- You have to keep doing all that miracle stuff.

MAKE A NAME FOR YOURSELF

As the new saint on the block, you're going to want to stand out. A big part of that is having a catchy, recognizable name like Joan of Arc, John the Baptist, Mother Teresa, or Cher.[*] If you have a common saint name, you may end up getting lost in the mix, and you don't want to be wandering around heaven saying, "Oh, you wanted Saint Brian R? Sorry, I'm Saint Brian P."

Some names really dominate in heaven. There are at least 148 saints named John, roughly 102 Peters, and over 40 Pauls, with a boatload more on deck. You've got at least a dozen Marys, and that doesn't even count your Marias and Maries. Think you're special because you're named Chad? Think again, hot shot. Saint Chad of seventh century Northumbria might have something to say about that.

Why so many dupes? Well, a lot of saints are from religious orders, and often when joining religious orders, you can choose to take on a new name in honor of a saint you admire. Combine that with the fact

---

[*] She's not a saint. Yet.

that Catholic families historically have named their children after saints, and you end up with a pretty small naming pool. If anything, it's a miracle there aren't more Chads.

If you're not willing to change your name and are worried it's not unique enough, there is one other option available: a cool nickname.

"Name's Saint Chad. 'Sup?" —Chad

HOLY NICKNAMES

lbert the Great. James the Lesser. Andrew the Apostle. For all of Catholic history, there have been saints who are distinguished by a nickname. Sometimes the nicknames are cool and sometimes they're not, but at the very least they're always memorable. If you're considering going the nickname route, here are a few that are already taken and a few that are completely made up. Can you spot the difference?

- Anastasius the Sinaite
- Basil the Great
- Ben the Fine
- Bede the Venerable
- Benedict the Vulnerable
- Charles the Netflix Subscriber
- David the Clammy
- Esther the Amazeballs
- Gabriel the Archangel
- Gregory the Illuminator
- Gregory of Nazianzus the Elder
- Isadore the Farmer
- John the Baptist
- John the Divine
- Julie the Hungry
- Julian the Hospitaller
- Leopold the Haberdasher
- Leo the Great

- Luke the Evangelist
- Macrina the Elder
- Macrina the Younger
- Macrina the Cougar
- Moses the Black
- Nancy the Fancy
- Paul the Fun
- Quincy the Side Sleeper
- Serapion the Scholastic
- Sebastian the Scholastic Book Fair
- Simon the Zealot
- Thomas the Outrageous
- Veronica the Late
- Walter the Lactose Intolerant

Don't forget to do your own: _____ the

YOUR NAME

_____
ADJECTIVE TO DESCRIBE YOU

ANSWER KEY

REAL: Anastasius the Sinaite, Basil the Great, Bede the Venerable, Gabriel the Archangel, Gregory the Illuminator, Gregory of Nazianus the Elder, Isadore the Farmer, John the Baptist, John the Divine, Julian the Hospitaller, Leo the Great, Luke the Evangelist, Macrina the Elder, Macrina the Younger, Moses the Black, Serapion the Scholastic, and Simon the Zealot.

JUST WISH THEY WERE REAL: The rest of them!

STEP 5
Saint You!

ou made it! You successfully died, proved you lived a life of heroic virtue, got the approval of bishops, cardinals, and the pope, did some miracles, and now, after surviving the religious equivalent of an audit, you're a saint! You may now proceed to the final step of sainthood: the rite of canonization. Your work is done and now it's time to party, Vatican style.

Don't get too excited. "Vatican style" means a mass. If you've never been to one, mass is about forty-five to sixty minutes of standing, sitting, kneeling, then standing and kneeling again. You recite prayers, listen to a sermon, sing songs, and, if you're lucky,* there might be a band with a guitar because you're the "hip" church. Toward the end of the service, you get a lil' cracker and a sip of Franzia. Also, the seats are called "pews," which is Latin for "my butt is numb."

The rite of canonization happens during a special mass said by the pope, usually in St. Peter's Square at the Vatican. The pope reads a special decree called the Formula of Canonization that officially

---

* Or unlucky, depending on the guitarist.

declares you to be a saint, and that's it! You're Saint You! Honestly, it feels a little anticlimactic given all you've done to get here. But hey, they also display a big banner with your face on it, so that part's pretty cool.

The Vatican pulls out all the stops when it's time to make a new saint. A canonization mass held by Pope Francis in St. Peter's Square in 2019 was attended by fifty thousand people. There are solo canonization masses, like for Saint Teresa of Calcutta (a.k.a. Mother Teresa) in 2016, but they are rare. Because canonization masses are such large, expensive events, you typically won't get one all to yourself. That massive celebration in 2019 was to canonize five new saints. But that pales in comparison to the largest ever canonization mass in 2013, where over eight hundred saints† were declared at the same time. Doesn't matter how devout the audience is, the surest way to lose a crowd is to have an old man‡ read a phone book's worth of names.

Now it's time to enjoy all the perks that come with a halo: churches—and maybe even cities—can be named after you, statues of you can be erected, you might become the patron of something, and you'll have a feast day that's celebrated by the worldwide church. You might also have your name taken by Catholic kids who are completing the sacrament of confirmation, which is the sacrament where you select a saint whose life you wish to venerate. This is fantastic news for anyone whose dream is to have a future thirteen-year-old spend a miserable Saturday writing a halfhearted essay about your life.

---

† They are the Martyrs of Otranto, an entire town that was slain in 1400s. Thankfully, an unusual occurrence.
‡ No matter who is currently pope, he is always an old man.

> **EQUIVALENT CANONIZATION**
> This is when the pope waives some or all miracle requirements and bumps you straight to halo-status. This has been invoked for saints like Hildegard of Bingen, Norbert, and Stephen of Hungary. You know how rich kids can get into Ivy League colleges with a C average and no extracurriculars? It's like that only for heaven.

Once your canonization mass is completed, you're free to relax and saint it up in heaven. You might want to perform a miracle every few years, just to keep things fresh. If it turns out you were fictional, you may end up getting removed from the liturgical calendar someday, but that's kind of it. Once you're a saint, you've got it made. Kick back, enjoy heaven, and check eBay every once in a while to see if you have any relics for sale on there.[*]

Of course, the main perk of becoming a saint is that you are officially, indisputably, in heaven. Now it's your turn to mentor the next generation of saints. Answer prayers, appear in visions, and intercede on behalf of us sinful meat sacks here on planet Earth. Or be a jerk and haunt people. Honestly up to you! You're already in heaven, what have you got to lose?

> **STEP 5: CHECKLIST**
> ✓ Enjoy the party!

---

[*] It's crazy out there. Put down this book right now and check it out.

You Want a Piece of Me? Relics!

Once you're a saint, your soul is officially in heaven. Your body is a different story. That stays on Earth, probably in a bunch of chopped-up pieces spread across the globe, because one of the most popular/creepy parts about sainthood is relics.

Relics are physical remnants of a saint's life. They are venerated as tangible reminders of the saint's virtues and of the fact that heaven is real and obtainable. But, the more fun reason relics are venerated is because Catholics believe they're imbued with the power of God, which means touching them could lead to a miracle. And, because Catholics love doing things in sets of three, there are actually three levels of relics.

Starting at the bottom, you've got third-class relics. This is any item, like a handkerchief or a book, that has touched a first-class relic (which we'll get to). A second-class relic is a personal possession the saint used in life. These are typically clothing, letters, prayer books, crosses, even furniture. Once you become a saint, anything you use daily could become a relic, so hide your vibrator.

First-class relics are the biggies. These aren't things that belonged to the saint, these *are* the saint. Bones, hair, vials of blood—whatever is left of you is fair game. There's no rest for the weary and no resting in peace for the saints. And if you think any part of you is off limits, consider that one of the most legendary relics of the Catholic Church is the Holy Prepuce a.k.a. Jesus's foreskin.[†]

[†] Sadly, it was stolen in the early 1980s and has been missing ever since. If you know the location of Jesus's foreskin, please call Crime Stoppers at 1-800-222-TIPS.

> **RELIQUARY**
>
> A reliquary is where you store remains. It's from the same root word as "relic" and in Latin means something along the lines of "remnant of the past." For example, your old Case Logic CD binder is a reliquary.

At this point you might be asking, "Why?" Or more accurately, "Jesus's foreskin?! Christ! WHY??" First, don't take the Lord's name in vain. Second, it all goes back to the origins of sainthood.

Remember how originally almost all saints were martyrs? Well, where is the most logical place to remember someone who died? Their grave. The tombs of martyrs became community centers of worship. As the Church strived to become more organized and concentrate power under bishops, churches were built on the sites of the most popular tombs. From the start, the physical remains of saints were at the center of organized worship. So much so, that today it is church law that all altars contain a relic of a saint. That means, if you've ever been inside of a Catholic Church, congratulations, you've been within spitting distance of a piece of somebody. Just ... don't spit.

> **TRANSLATION**
>
> In the world of saints, translation means moving a body or relic of human remains from one place to another, as in "we translated the hand of that saint from the graveyard to a cool gold reliquary." Translation usually involves some degree of prayer and ceremony because, ya know, Catholics.

The popularity of relics helped the Church establish itself in the early years, but it also led to some weird shit, like the relics black market. People have always been willing to pay a lot for miracles,[*] and other people have always been willing to take advantage of that first group. Prior to the discovery of DNA, it was almost impossible to tell what bones[†] belonged to what person, so if I told you I had a femur that belonged to Saint Patrick and you wanted to believe me, you probably would. Even some members of the clergy participated in the black market, knowing that cooler relics would draw more worshipers to their flock. It's why the Church works so hard now to authenticate relics.[‡] It's also why there are four heads of John the Baptist floating around.[§] If you want to stay popular long after you're gone, you're

---

[*] How much did you spend on lottery tickets this year?
[†] Or foreskins.
[‡] You can't display a relic without a certificate of authenticity, like how the MLB authenticates official game bats.
[§] John baptized Jesus and was possibly his cousin, so when he was beheaded, his skull became the hottest relic around. It was the Birkin bag of human remains. In addition to at least four places claiming to have his skull, an additional two claim to have portions of his skull. So best-case scenario: John the Baptist had six heads.

going to have to leave behind some sick relics and, for bonus points, have them put in some sick reliquaries. Catholic pilgrims and regular ole tourists will travel from far and wide to see a real (formerly) live piece of you. For inspiration, here are some badass relics from your soon-to-be saintly peers.

Saint Teresa of Avila's Hand

Santa Teresa Chapel, Spain

Look familiar? It's long been rumored that the design of Marvel's Infinity Gauntlet was inspired by the reliquary containing the hand of Saint Teresa of Avila. In life, Teresa was famous for having mystic visions, writing several books, and founding a strict order of nuns called the Discalced Carmelites. After her death, her body was incorrupt and split up into several pieces, including this hand, which was placed in a jeweled reliquary, making her the only saint who is unofficially part of the MCU.

"I. Am. Saint Teresa of Avila!"

Saint Anthony's Jaw and Tongue

Basilica of Saint Anthony of Padua, Italy

Saint Anthony was a famous orator who spent his life traveling thirteenth-century Europe to give sermons and spread the word of God. So, it makes sense that his most famous relics are his jaw and tongue, which are on display in separate reliquaries for some reason. When priests opened Saint Anthony's coffin years after his death, they found that the body had decomposed but the tongue was preserved. Despite the fact that a juicy tongue in a decomposed body is somehow creepier than a decomposed tongue in a juicy body, the priests were pumped and today the tongue remains a strong tourist destination.

Saint Catherine of Siena's Whole Damn Head

Basilica San Domenico, Italy

While you're in Italy visiting Saint Anthony's jaw and tongue, pop over to Siena to see Saint Catherine's head. The only thing more bizarre than seeing a mounted saint head is the story of how it got there. Legend says that, after her death, representatives from Catherine's hometown of Siena wanted to lay her to rest there. Folks from Rome, where she died, disagreed. In what

Brow game still on point.

might be the worst heist in history, worshipers snuck into Rome to smuggle the body out, only afterward realizing that a whole body is hard to smuggle. So, they did the logical thing: cut off her head and just took that. Creepy outcome, but bonus points for creative problem-solving!

Saint Bernadette's Entire Freaking Body
Nevers, France

Any saint can leave behind a cool head or tongue, but it takes a pro to leave behind a whole incorrupt (-ish) body. After Saint Bernadette died in 1879, her body was exhumed three times to confirm that it was incorrupt. It was then placed in a special reliquary at her convent in France. However, in the early twentieth century, officials decided to place a wax mask over her face and hands because the body was turning black with patches of mildew (a.k.a. corrupt). Bernadette is still deemed technically incorrupt because the damage to her body is blamed on human interference after her exhumation, not on natural decay. Basically, if humans had never peeked into her coffin, Bernadette might still be incorrupt, which makes her Schrodinger's saint.

Saint Januarius's Blood
Cathedral of Saint Januarius, Italy

Vials of saint blood aren't that uncommon (which is in and of itself a gross thing to say), but what makes Saint Januarius's blood special is that it occasionally and miraculously liquefies, despite the fact that Januarius died in 305 CE. The blood is said to liquefy three times a year and, when it doesn't, it's taken as a bad omen. Maybe that's not true, but it did fail to liquefy in 2020, so maybe it is!*

---

*   This obviously predicted the most famous tragedy of 2020: the delay of the release of the ninth installment of the Fast & Furious franchise, *F9*.

Make Your Own Relic

Now that you're a saint (or well on your way), relics of your body are going to be a hot commodity. If you're worried that your corpse alone might not be enough, use the space below to create some homemade relics. For bonus points, hide this page with no context someplace where a future family member will find it and be creeped out.

Lick This Page (Your holy spit might be valuable in the future. It's also a great way to call dibs on this book so nobody else can take it.)

Tape a Piece of Your Hair Here:

Tape Nail Clippings Here (Bonus Points for a Tooth!):

Go Watch *WALL-E*,* Then Deposit Authentic Saint Tears Here:

Make Your Own Holy Card

Saints and almost-saints get the ultimate Catholic collectible: a holy card. Holy cards have tons of great uses: bookmarks, fake credit cards in old wallets for kids to play with, and probably other things, too!

A standard holy card has an image of a saint on the front and a prayer plus basic saint stats (dates they lived, feast day, batting average, etc.) on the back. People often carry a holy card for a patron saint so they can more easily pray on-the-go. Holy cards have been around since the fifteenth century but really hit their stride in the mid-1800s when mass printing became affordable and a critical mass of people could actually read.

There are multiple types of holy cards, including ones for established saints and ones for saints-to-be. If you're a saint, your holy card

---

* Watching *Up* or *Coco* is also acceptable.

is a useful prayer aid and keepsake. If you're a saint-to-be, your holy card is important marketing material. Remember, you can't advance in the canonization process without a confirmed miracle, and you can't perform miracles if people don't pray to you. Holy cards with prayers written on them encourage people to pray to potential saints for intercession. Think of them like heaven's rookie cards.

So, if you don't already have one, now's the time. Fill in the blanks below to make your very own Vatican-approved[†] holy card!

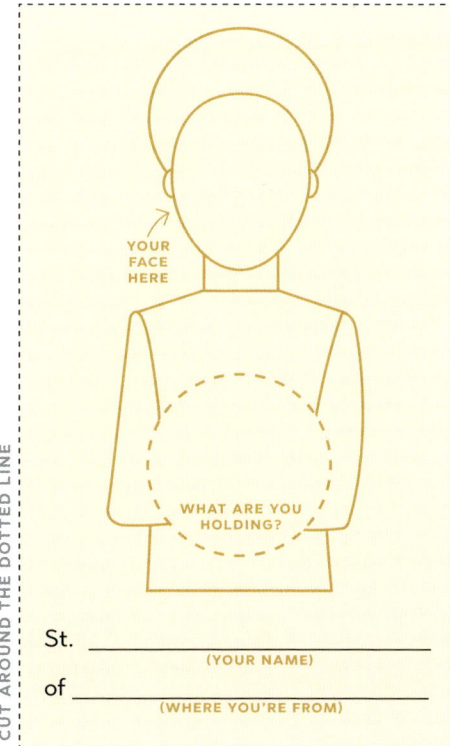

Patron Saint of _____
(WHAT'S YOUR CAUSE?)

Pray for us...

Dear St. _____,
(YOUR NAME)
protector of _____,
(NOUN)
lover of _____,
(NOUN)
guide us _____
(ADVERB)
and help us through our _____
(ADJECTIVE)
lives. And when our _____
(ADJECTIVE)
days are through, let us enjoy heaven with you and _____.
(CELEBRITY)
Amen.

Feast Day _____
(WHEN DO YOU THINK YOU'LL DIE?)

CUT AROUND THE DOTTED LINE

NORMALLY CUTTING A PAGE OUT OF A BOOK IS A SIN, BUT I ABSOLVE YOU!

---

† Very much not Vatican approved.

Saints Who Walked Six Miles after Being Beheaded

Saint Denis (d. c. 258)

He doesn't really fit into any other category, but this book would be remiss to allow you to enter the gates of heaven without knowing about Saint Denis. Denis was Bishop of Paris, who, along with a few of his colleagues, was sent on a mission to convert some pagans. Not much is known about Denis's career, but it's assumed he was martyred as part of an anti-Christian sweep by the Roman emperor. He was probably a very good bishop and cared for his people and blah blah blah but also HE CARRIED HIS DECAPITATED HEAD FOR SIX MILES. After being beheaded on Montmartre, Denis picked up his noggin and hoofed it over to the burbs. A basilica in his honor was erected on the spot where he stopped walking. This story didn't come about until hundreds of years after Denis was martyred—which means for pretty obvious reasons it's probably not true—but it's

"AND my eyes are shut!" —Denis

worth including because walking a 10K is impressive, but doing it while carrying your lopped-off head is legendary.

STEP 5 COMPLETE!
Achievement Unlocked: Saint

THE PROS:
- You're a saint!
- You're now officially in heaven's cool kids club. Being popular on Earth is great, so being popular in heaven must be *amazing*.
- Sainthood comes with major perks: a halo, holy cards, medals, churches named after you, kids named after you—you might even get a city named after you.

THE CONS:
- Your body will probably get split up into bits and pieces and spread around the globe.
- You have to do shifts in heaven's call center to hear prayers and decide when to intercede and kick something up the chain to God. Nobody knows exactly how this works, so let's assume it's a telethon setup.

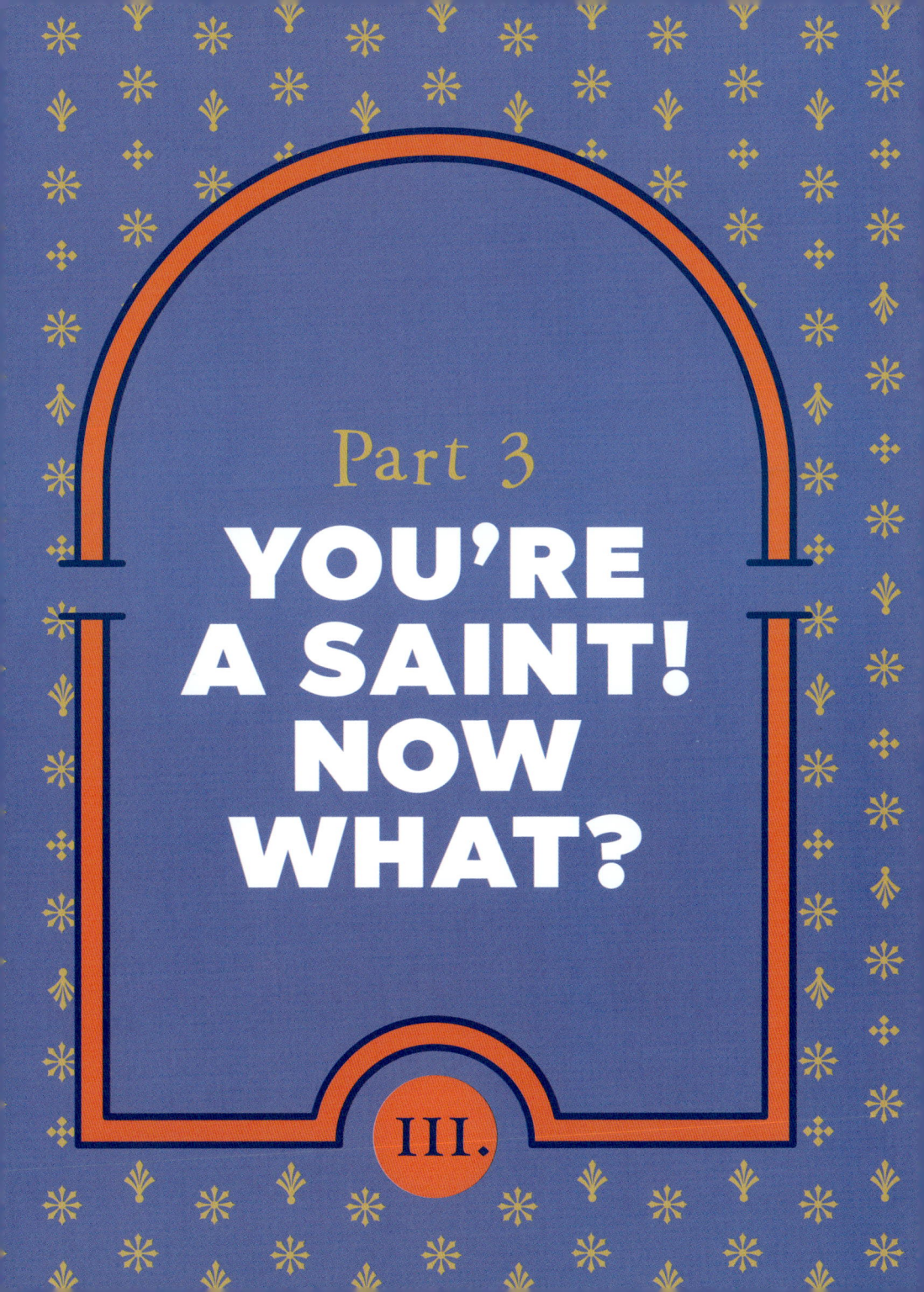

ANOTHER LETTER FROM GOD

Dear Saint,

Congratulations on your acceptance into heaven as an official Catholic saint! We're happy to have you and hope you enjoy your stay. You have a cloud reserved between your family (only the members you liked) and every celebrity you found hot, preserved at the age at which you found them most hot. You're welcome.

    As an official saint, you are expected to intercede on behalf of humans, grant the occasional miracle, and attend the weekly saint potluck. This Thursday is casseroles. Don't try to pass off something store bought. I'm God. I'll notice.

    Saint Peter, who is in charge of general admin, will set you up with the basics: your keycard for the Pearly Gates, the Wi-Fi password, pool hours, etc. Other than that, make yourself at home. A choir of angels will show you to your parking spot.

    My office door is always open if you want to chat. To get a few of the most common questions out of the way: no, there is no "right" religion; despite what you've seen in paintings, my son was not a

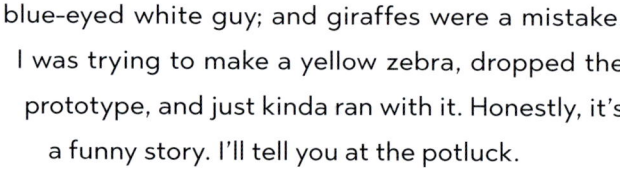

blue-eyed white guy; and giraffes were a mistake. I was trying to make a yellow zebra, dropped the prototype, and just kinda ran with it. Honestly, it's a funny story. I'll tell you at the potluck.

We in heaven appreciate your dedication to completing the canonization process (which, by the way, I didn't design. My version would've been more of an *American Ninja Warrior*–style obstacle course. Humans always overthink this stuff.) Welcome aboard, and we look forward to seeing you achieve great things in your new role.

—God

P. S. I'm not real.
P. P. S. Just kidding!
P. P. P. S. Or am I???

You've done it! You are officially a USDA Grade A certified Catholic saint. The process took decades, if not centuries, and most people who helped you get your halo are probably now also dead and in heaven with you. But they probably aren't canonized saints. Awkward.

Now you get to live out eternity on Santa's Nice List.[*] But as you've seen, there are plenty of saints who have gone into obscurity faster than the Nintendo GameCube. How do you avoid being a Saint Anthelm or Saint Zosimus?[†] You have to make sure your story lives on. That could be by attaching your name to schools, cities, or holidays, or by making sure your image is captured in paintings or sculptures. You could always pop down to work a few miracles, but if that seems like too much work, you could just try to become a patron saint of something popular like cookies or naps.

As a saint, the universe is your oyster, but first, you should get the lay of the land. And since this is heaven, the land is clouds.

---

[*] And you now know Santa personally. Very cool!
[†] Saint Anthelm was a twelfth-century monk and bishop, and Saint Zosimus was a fifth-century pope. Both were probably lovely guys, but they aren't exactly topping the charts anymore.

KNOW YOUR WAY AROUND HEAVEN

- **Saint You:** That's you!
- **Pearly Gates:** According to the Bible, heaven has twelve gates, each made of a single pearl. It also says the streets of heaven are "pure gold, transparent as glass," so be sure to wear shoes with good grip.
- **Clouds:** Based on every painting of heaven, there's no furniture, only clouds. It's basically a city made of beanbag chairs, which honestly does sound like heaven.
- **God:** Humanity's best guess is that God looks like either buff Santa, a ray of light, or Morgan Freeman.
- **Jesus:** The boss's son. Be nice. Don't mention his foreskin.
- **The Holy Spirit:** This is the spirit of God that enters humans who have faith. Most famously depicted in the Bible as tongues of fire. Also known as the Holy Ghost. Spooky!
- **Other Saints:** Say hi! Learn the secret handshake!
- **Other Dead People:** Remember, everyone who dies and goes to heaven is technically a saint. But they are way less likely to have a toe in an altar in Hartford. Hopefully.

- **Angels:** God's servants and messengers. Entry-level work, but they get wings, so it's a wash.
- **Archangels:** These are the top angels. The warriors in the battle of good versus evil. They have wings and swords and vacillate between wearing flowy robes and armor. Try to befriend them.
- **Cherubs:** God's attendants. Typically depicted in art as cute lil' chubby babies.
- **Seraphim:** A choir of angels who stay close to God's throne. They each have six wings, which feels very show-offy.

CITY SAINTS, COUNTRY SAINTS

City Saints

Saints are honored in many ways, but one of the biggest is having cities named after them. If you want to make sure your legacy is rock-solid, you'll want to try to join their ranks. Here are a few examples of saints who really put themselves on the map.[*]

St. Louis, Missouri: St. Louis was named after the French king and saint by a French fur trader named Pierre Laclède. The city attracted so many Catholics early on that it earned the nicknamed the Rome of the West. It's also why so many people now call Rome the St. Louis of the East.[†]

St. Augustine, Florida: Spanish sailor Don Pedro Menéndez first spotted land in Florida on August 28, 1565, which is the feast day of Saint Augustine. But it took him and his sailors a week to actually step foot on land because they had trouble finding parking. Once they did, they held a mass and named the area St. Augustine. It seems unlikely

---

[*] This list is restricted to U.S. cities, but this phenomenon exists across the globe. Don't believe it? Buy a globe!
[†] Okay fine, no people say this, but maybe we should start!

that the indigenous people who already lived there got a vote in the name change.

St. Paul, Minnesota: Originally, St. Paul was named Pig's Eye Landing after the unfortunately named Pierre "Pig's Eye" Parrant. A few years later, a priest built a church in the town called St. Paul's. Folks seemed to agree that that was a way better name, so they changed it. Rough day for ole Pig's Eye.

San Diego, California: San Diego is named after Saint Diego de Alcalá de Henares a.k.a. Saint Didacus, who was a Franciscan friar and hermit. So, of course he is now the namesake of a city most famous for having big, crowded amusement parks. Most hermits would dislike SeaWorld.

San Antonio, Texas: San Antonio was named after Saint Anthony of Padua in the late seventeenth century. Anthony is the patron saint against shipwrecks, which should come in handy the next time you hit the high seas at the SeaWorld.‡

Santa Fe, New Mexico: Technically the full name of this city is Villa Real de la Santa Fé de San Francisco Asis in honor of Saint Francis of Assisi. But that's really long, so residents switched to calling it Santa Fe, which translates to "Holy shit, that other name was way too long."§

---

‡   Yes, that is two SeaWorld references in a row. And they said it couldn't be done!
§   Actually, it translates to "Holy Faith," but this is definitely implied.

Country Saints

Many Caribbean islands are named after saints by the explorers who "discovered" them. Here are just a few.

Saint Lucia: Named after Saint Lucy, whose feast day is December 13, which is also the date when, according to legend, French sailors landed there. Okay, "landed" is generous. They shipwrecked. So, they "discovered" Saint Lucia in the same way you trip and fall down the stairs and "discover" the basement floor.

Virgin Islands: Named after Saint Ursula and her ship full of eleven thousand virgins, who, as you may remember from earlier in the book, probably weren't real.

Saint Kitts: Named in honor of Saint Christopher, the patron saint of travelers. But it was named by Christopher Columbus, so it's really in honor of himself. He also named Saint Barts after his brother, who wasn't a saint. Just a guy named Bart. Turns out Chris was not the best guy.

Honorable Mentions

These cities aren't named after saints, but their names are still Catholic as hell.

Sacramento, California: Sacramento is Spanish for the word "sacrament," so it's very Catholic but also very unoriginal. This is the religious equivalent of naming your dog Woof.

Los Angeles, California: Los Angeles is Spanish for "the angels," but the original name for the city was…something different. Historians dispute the actual first name, with almost twelve variations in play, from the straightforward Ciudad de los Angeles to the mouthful of El Pueblo de Nuestra Senora la Reyna de los Angeles del Rio Porciuncula. If you're curious what the other possible first names are, feel free to Google them the next time you're standing still on the 405.

Holy Cross, Alaska: In the 1880s, nonnative Alaskans settled in a town called Askhomute. At some point between then and 1912, they said, "no we didn't" and renamed the town Holy Cross.

SAINTS YOU CAN EAT

ow that you're officially Saint You, Catholics all across the globe will (hopefully) celebrate and venerate you in a variety of ways: holy cards, medals, churches named after you, kids named after you, and, if you're lucky, tasty treats named after you. Break out the butter and preheat your oven to 350°, because it's time to meet the select few saints who are honored via pastry.

Saint Honoré Cake

This zillion-calorie treat is appropriately named after Saint Honoré, the patron saint of bakers and pastry chefs. Honoré was a bishop in France during the sixth century. It's unclear whether he himself was ever a baker, but legend says that on the day he was named bishop, a baker's peel (the paddle used to take loaves out of the oven) somehow ended up in the ground and transformed into a tree. Seems like that should've made him the patron saint of spontaneous trees, but the bakers snagged him first. In the nineteenth century, French bakers honored Honoré with a puff pastry topped with vanilla custard, choux pastry, and caramelized sugar. In the twenty-first century, Saint Honoré was further honored by having his pastry be the technical challenge on Series 10 Week 9 of the *Great British Bake Off*.*

Lussekatter

These tasty little Swedish rolls are also known as Saint Lucia buns in honor of Saint Lucy. You might remember Lucy from the chapter on virgin martyrs. She's the one who pulled the ultimate "go big or go home" move, by plucking out her eyes and presenting them to her betrothed on a tray. Well, at some point some baker must have heard that story and thought, *Hey, cool idea for a pastry!* Because today, Lucy, who is the patron saint of blindness, is honored with saffron buns shaped like curled up cats (cute) topped with either currants or raisins to look like eyeballs (terrifying).

Hildegardplätzchen

These are the only treats on this list with the distinction of actually having been invented by the saint they are named after. In addition to writing poems, music, letters, and her own freaking language, multi-hyphenate Saint Hildegard of Bingen also wrote several recipes. Hildegard lived smack in the middle of the medieval era, so her recipes sought to correct imbalances of the four humors: blood (outgoing, positive), yellow bile (irritable), black bile (melancholy), and phlegm (calm). Her Hildegardplätzchen a.k.a. "cookies of joy" contain spices like nutmeg, cinnamon, and cloves to correct for too much of that

---

* Rosie won.

black bile melancholy. Meaning, on top of all her other achievements, Saint Hildegard was the first person to officially crack the equation of cookies + eating them = happy.

Yemas de Santa Teresa

These desserts are named after Saint Teresa of Avila, and unfortunately that's kind of the whole story. Nobody knows for sure where they came from. They seem to have been around Spain since the medieval era and became popular in the mid-nineteenth century. Since wineries used to use egg whites in the wine-making process, they often gave the yolks to local convents for baking. So, one theory is that these treats were invented by the nuns at the convent in Avila, since *yemas* is Spanish for "yolks." Other than that, the only connection between these treats and Saint Teresa is that she was an EGG-cellent saint.

Zeppole di San Giuseppe

In Italian, San Giuseppe is Saint Joseph a.k.a. Mary's husband a.k.a. Jesus's stepfather. Much like yemas de Santa Teresa, evidence of an actual connection between the dessert and Saint Joseph is slim to none. The best shred of evidence seems to be a legend that, in order to earn money during their flight to Egypt, Joseph made ends meet by selling fritters. That would make Jesus's biological dad God and his stepdad a doughnut maker, which really seems like a win-win.

Vasilopita

Vasilopita is a traditional Greek Orthodox cake, but the saint it's named after is venerated by the Roman Catholic Church as well. In the fourth century, archbishop Basil the Great was asked by the emperor to collect a tax on his people. Knowing how poor his followers were, Basil refused, and prayed for God to intervene. Well, he's Basil the Great, not Basil the Just Okay, so of course God did intervene and moved the emperor to return all the previously paid taxes to the city. A chest of gold and jewels was given to Basil to return to his people. Well, he's Basil the Great, not Basil the Accountant, so he had no idea what belonged to whom. Basil did the only logical thing and baked all the money into a big bread, then invited everyone in town to come grab a piece. Miraculously, everyone grabbed pieces containing exactly what they were owed. That's why "vasilopita" translates to "Saint Basil's Bread." It's also why you should think twice about biting into a piece of it, because you might chip your tooth on a gold coin.

SAINTS WHO PUT THE "CHRIST" BACK IN "HAPPY HOLIDAYS"

It's one thing to be a famous saint among Catholics. It's a whole other level to be a famous saint among everybody else. There are only a handful of saints who have managed to bridge the gap between religious and secular devotion, but the ones who have are truly legendary. If you want to achieve ultimate saint fame, you need to get yourself associated with a major holiday. But don't worry, as you'll see from these saints, the connection can be tenuous at best.

February 14, Valentine's Day

Most of what we know about Saint Valentine's life is probably exaggerated, which honestly fits for a holiday about declarations of love. The real Valentine lived in Rome in the third century, where he was imprisoned for refusing to worship the Roman gods. From here, there are two competing stories about his fate. The first is that he miraculously restored the sight of his jailer's daughter, who was blind. Then, on the way to his execution, he sent the now not-blind daughter a goodbye message signed, "from your Valentine." The second story is that the Roman emperor Claudius II banned marriage because he was having a tough time recruiting young soldiers. Our hopeless romantic Valentine decided to marry couples in secret in defiance of the emperor. This version of the story also ends with him being executed. However, there is a third story: February 14 was already the Roman feast of Juno, the goddess of love, and switching that date over to Saint Valentine's feast day was a way of gobbling up a pagan festival and turning it Christian. Less romantic? Yes. Probable? Probably.

March 17, Saint Patrick's Day

Saint Patrick's Day is the sacred feast of public intoxication. The man it's based on, Saint Patrick, is the patron saint of Ireland, which is pretty impressive since Patrick wasn't even Irish. He was born in Roman Britain and was kidnapped and enslaved by the Irish at age sixteen. He eventually found his way home, became a bishop, and decided to return to Ireland as a missionary. Legend says that he converted tons of people to Christianity and that he drove all the snakes out of Ireland, which must have been easy, since snakes aren't indigenous to Ireland. It would sort of be like bragging that you drove all the Yankees fans out of Boston. Today, Patrick is honored by overusing green food dye and puking on the sidewalk by 2:00 p.m.

December 25, Christmas

Okay, technically Christmas is all about Jesus, who is not a saint. But there's a reason Jesus's face isn't on the Coke can—in the United States, the real star of Christmas is Santa Claus a.k.a. Saint Nick.

Much like Valentine, a hefty amount of the true story of Nicholas is legend. The only thing we know for sure about the real Nick is that he was a bishop in the fourth century. There are stories of him being an extremely generous gift-giver and even throwing bags of gold through the windows of the homes of young women who couldn't afford dowries. The stories got blown up from there: reindeer got added at some point, a fondness for milk and cookies, a few elves got thrown into the mix, and bing bang boom, you've got Santa.

THE GAME OF (AFTER)LIFE

ooks are heavy, so if you don't want to carry this guide around, just tear out these pages and carry them around with you to keep track of your progress to heaven.

- ✓ Get baptized. This puts you officially on Team Catholic. You'll need evidence of your baptism to be canonized, so remember: pics or it didn't happen.
- ✓ Lead a life of heroic virtue.
- ✓ Make sure people know how heroically virtuous you are. Get good at posting humble brags to social media.
- ✓ BONUS POINTS: Levitate, bilocate, have the stigmata, or do other cool physical stuff like that thing where you can curl your tongue three times.
- ✓ Die. This one's easy. Everyone can and will do it.
- ✓ Stay dead for at least five years. Also, fairly easy.
- ✓ BONUS POINTS: Don't let your corpse decay. Maybe emit a sweet smell. Try swallowing a car air freshener right before you kick the bucket.

- ✓ Living people decide you should be a saint. Maybe drop some hints like, "Guys, wouldn't it be CRAZY if you decided I should be a saint after I died?"
- ✓ A bishop opens an investigation into your life. Hope you deleted your browser history before dying.
- ✓ FIRST NEW TITLE: SERVANT OF GOD!
- ✓ A team, coordinated by your bishop, investigates your whole damn life.
- ✓ The team interviews anyone who knew you, so be nice or start bribing.
- ✓ The team gathers up everything you ever wrote. Time to burn your *Twilight* fan fic.
- ✓ All your info gets sent to Rome via snail mail. Pay the extra postage for signed delivery.
- ✓ The head of your team (the postulator) moves to Rome to continue working. With the time zone change, your cause is now one day in the future!
- ✓ The Vatican's Dicastery for the Causes of Saints investigates you all over again.
- ✓ Your cause gets assigned a relator who helps your postulator write a *positio*—a big document talking about how great you are. It's like a Tinder profile written by someone else.
- ✓ Take a little nap. This process takes forever, and you deserve a break.
- ✓ A group of theologians examine your *positio*. If they approve, then...

- ✓ A group of bishops and cardinals examine your *positio*. If they approve, then...
- ✓ The pope examines your *positio*. If he approves, then...
- ✓ SECOND NEW TITLE: VENERABLE!
- ✓ SPLIT IN THE ROAD: If you are a martyr, proceed straight to BLESSED. If you died regular style, continue.
- ✓ Perform at least one miracle. Preferably a medical miracle. Helping the Cleveland Guardians win a World Series would be appreciated but probably won't count.
- ✓ A group of doctors called the Consulta Medica reviews your miracle to see if there's any scientific explanation. Your best bet is to cure something that medical science doesn't know much about yet, like menopause or why copays exist.
- ✓ A group of theologians double-checks that your miracle was done by you and not some other wannabe saint.
- ✓ NEW TITLE: BLESSED!
- ✓ You know how you just did a miracle? Do another. (Or, if you were martyred, do your first miracle.)
- ✓ ULTIMATE TITLE: SAINT!
- ✓ Collect one (1) halo and proceed directly to heaven's VIP lounge.

CERTIFICATE OF SAINTIFICATION

Congratulations on two major accomplishments: (1) reading an entire book and (2) achieving sainthood. Your reward for the latter will be eternal paradise in heaven. Your reward for the former is this fun certificate that you can cut out and hang up to impress all your friends!

QUICK TIMELINE OF THE HISTORY OF CANONIZATION

6-4 B.C.
MAYBE? NOBODY IS TOTALLY SURE: Jesus is born.

787: The Second Council of Nicea declares a bunch of stuff, including that every altar must contain the relics of a saint.

1582: Pope Gregory XIII drops the Gregorian calendar, which fixes a problem with leap years and means all the dates before this on the timeline are kind of best guesses. Oops!

33: Jesus dies. Christianity is born.

1234: Gregory IX publishes the *Decretals*, formally saying only a pope has the right to declare someone a saint.

1588: Pope Sixtus V establishes the Sacred Congregation of Rites, which eventually becomes the present-day Congregation for the Causes of Saints.

1765: Joseph Priestley invents the modern timeline. Thanks, Joe!

1969: Pope Paul VI creates the Congregation for the Causes of Saints and officially removes fictional saints from the Roman calendar.

1642: Pope Urban VII decrees that candidates for sainthood must demonstrate heroic virtues.

1917: The Code of Canon Law is published, which codifies procedures for beatification and canonization.

1983: Pope John Paul streamlines the canonization process by reducing the number of required miracles to two and the number of years before the process can begin to five. Also *Return of the Jedi* comes out.

GLOSSARY

There are lots of words in Catholicism. Here are some of them!

ALL SAINTS' DAY: All Saints' Day is celebrated on November 1 every year and is the feast of every saint in heaven, not just the canonized ones. Remember, everyone in heaven is technically a saint. So this feast day is for everyone from Saint Patrick to your nana (one hopes). It's the all-staff holiday party of feast days. Hopefully the boss's speech is short.

ANGELS: Angels are heavenly beings created by God. They were made first, kind of like a rough draft for humans (definitely don't say that to their faces). Angels can be saints, but saints can't be angels. Fallen angels are demons, the most famous of which is Satan a.k.a. Lucifer a.k.a. the Devil a.k.a. the Prince of Darkness. There are nine choirs (types) of angels in heaven, each with different jobs and social ranking. They are: seraphim, cherubim, thrones, dominions, virtues, powers, principalities, archangels, angels, and David Boreanaz.

APOSTLE: Technically, anybody who spreads the word of God, but usually used to mean the Twelve Apostles who were Jesus's original crew. Their main miracle was keeping a friend group of that size together before the invention of the group chat.

BISHOPS: Bishops oversee multiple churches in a geographical area. They're considered the successors of the Twelve Apostles because they are spread across the globe making sure the Church runs well. Bishops are usually chosen from local priests and selected by the pope. Some especially large and especially Catholic areas might have an archbishop who oversees multiple bishops. Only bishops are eligible to become cardinals, so there is room for promotion!

CARDINALS: Cardinals are the step below the pope and monitor dioceses around the world. There are just over two hundred cardinals globally, and they have to meet with the pope at least once every five years to make sure he's up to speed on the global church. Cardinals are the only ones eligible to become pope and the College of Cardinals selects every new pope. Plus, they traditionally wear red, which is a fun pop of color.

CATECHISM: The Catechism is the official teachings of the Catholic Church. It covers everything from basic beliefs and the sacraments to the Ten Commandments and how to pray. It's the instruction manual for Catholicism. It's basically the "How to Be a Catholic" section of this book but with significantly fewer jokes.

CATHEDRAL: The principal church of a diocese, presided over by the bishop. Usually extra pretty. Sometimes has a gift shop!

COMMUNION OF SAINTS: The concept that all souls, both alive and dead, are united in God's love. It draws attention to the connection between the living and the dead via prayer. The only people not in the communion of saints are souls in hell. Sorry guys! You had your shot!

DENOMINATION: Denominations are groups who share the same overall religion but differ in practice and beliefs. For example, Roman Catholic and Protestant are both denominations of Christianity, and Tobey Maguire and Tom Holland are both denominations of Spiderman.

DIOCESE: A diocese is the geographical area under the jurisdiction of a bishop. A priest is in charge of a church; a bishop is in charge of a diocese, which contains multiple churches; and the pope is in charge of everybody.

DOGMA: Church doctrine that is indisputable because it has been revealed by God. For example, the idea of Immaculate Conception (that Mary was free from original sin when she conceived). Also, a fun Kevin Smith movie.

ENCYCLICAL: A letter written by the pope to clarify a teaching of the Church. Used whenever the Church needs an OS update.

EXCOMMUNICATION: The process by which somebody is booted from the Church community. You lose all your Catholic membership perks, like the free sip of wine every Sunday.

GENUFLECTION: The act of bending at the knee to show reverence, typically for the Eucharist. It's a teeny, little glute workout for the Lord.

GLOSSARY: A list of terms that are kind of interesting and useful to know but don't really fit anywhere else in the book. Also used at the end of books to make them seem smart.

HOLY DAYS OF OBLIGATION: Special days (in addition to every Sunday) when Catholics are required to attend church services unless they are busy, or forget, or are out of town, or don't feel like it.

PAPAL INFALLIBILITY: Papal infallibility means that the pope cannot make a mistake when it comes to morals or faith when speaking *ex cathedra*, which is Latin for "from the chair." In this case "the chair" means the Chair of Saint Peter a.k.a. the first pope, which sits in the Vatican. Of course, this is symbolic. The pope doesn't have to literally be sitting in the chair to proclaim something that's infallible. He can be in any position he wants. Basically, papal infallibility means that, when it comes to doctrine (including canonization), whatever the pope says, goes. The concept of papal infallibility has been around for centuries, but it wasn't officially defined until the nineteenth century. Also, the chair is probably not old enough to have ever touched the butt of Saint Peter.

PRIESTS: Priests are the local-level Catholic leaders. They say Mass, deliver sacraments, occasionally teach, and oversee individual churches. The word "priest" is derived from the Latin *presbyter*, which means "elder," which is fitting since fewer and fewer young people actually want to become priests.

SACRILEGE: Irreverence toward people, places, or things associated with God. (*See this book.*)

THE HOLY TRINITY: The Holy Trinity describes the fact that God the Father, Jesus, and the Holy Spirit are three beings in one. None is above the other. It's kind of like how you have the version of yourself at work, the version of yourself relaxing at home, and the version of yourself on a date. They're all you, but they are very separate and have different rules about when it's okay to unbutton your pants.

TITHING: Tithing, derived from the word "tenth," is the practice of giving one-tenth of your income to the Church. It used to be mandatory, like taxes. Now it's optional, like taxes for the wealthy.

TRANSUBSTANTIATION: Catholics believe that, once consecrated, the bread and wine of the Eucharist becomes the body and blood of Jesus Christ. It still looks like bread and wine, but its substance has changed. This symbolizes the sacrifice Jesus made for the world and that, with enough faith, even Franzia can change.

TRANSVERBERATION: A mystical experience by which someone's heart and/or soul is pierced by God's love. It's sometimes described as feeling like a dart, arrow, or spear literally going through the body. A totally nonsexual, ecstatic penetration that has definitely no connection to the Church's repressive history toward sexuality.

YAHWEH: The name of God as told to Moses. Means "I am who I am" in ancient Hebrew. The Latinized version is Jehovah, which, if you're ever in an *Indiana Jones and the Last Crusade* situation, remember, in Latin, Jehovah begins with an "I".

YOU: A saint! Woohoo!

ACKNOWLEDGMENTS

I'd like to start off by thanking God, who hopefully has a fantastic sense of humor. I also need to thank my parents, John David and Susan for sending me to Catholic school and making our local library feel like a second home. I'm endlessly grateful to my sister, Diana, for reading all my silly stories, giving me good notes, and letting me copy her confirmation workbook when we were kids.

This book wouldn't exist without the support of everyone at Sourcebooks, my dedicated editor, Kate Roddy, and my wonderful literary agent, Kate Mack at Aevitas. Go Team Kate! Also huge thanks to my managers Maggie Haskins and Casey Neumeier at Artists First and my agent Jonathan Levy at UTA for encouraging me to write this book back when it was just a half idea in an email. Thank you to Stephen Colbert, Tom Purcell, and everyone at *The Late Show* for making me funnier every day.

I'm lucky to have fantastic, smart, funny friends who gave encouragement and notes at various points of this process: Kristen Bartlett, Nicole Conlan, Ariel Dumas, Michael Cruz Kayne,

Eliana Kwartler, and Gloria Teal. You are all so talented it makes me furious.

I started writing this book proposal while pregnant with our first child. Now, I'm finishing up final edits while holding our second. I could not have done this without my wonderful, happy, goofy babies. Thank you for being good sleepers so mommy can write.

Finally, I have to thank my husband Joe Leonardo, Jr. He read every draft, listened to every pitch (both good and bad), and was willing to talk endlessly about obscure Catholic history. Joe, you're an amazing husband, a fantastic dad, and the funniest person I know. Thank you for having faith in me.

BIBLIOGRAPHY

Hi! It's me. The person who wrote this book. I hope you liked it and are now happily on your path to heaven. Maybe you learned some fun facts that you can use to get on *Jeopardy!* or show off at parties. If you did, great! But anything in this book that seemed remotely intelligent exists because of research drawn from books and articles written by people much smarter (albeit less funny) than me. If you want to know more about any of this stuff, you should check out their work.* Then you'll know enough to win at *Jeopardy!* and be excruciatingly boring at dinner parties.

"American Saints and Blesseds." United States Conference of Catholic Bishops. Accessed September 15, 2022. https://www.usccb.org/prayer-and-worship/prayers-and-devotions/saints/american-saints-and-blesseds.

"An Early History of Saint Paul." Visit Saint Paul. Accessed November 6, 2022. https://www.visisaintpaul.com/blog/an-early-history-of-saint-paul/.

Archer, Peter. *Religion 101: From Allah to Zen Buddhism, an Exploration of the Key People, Practices, and Beliefs That Have Shaped the Religions of the World.* New York: Adams Media, 2013.

Baring-Gould, Sabine. *The Lives of the Saints, Volume II.* London: Ballantyne Press. Project Gutenberg, May 12, 2014. https://www.gutenberg.org/files/45604/45604-h/45604-h.htm.

---

* From a library or independent bookstore if you want to earn extra heaven points.

Beam, Christopher. "How Would the Pope Self-Flagellate?" *Slate*. January 26, 2010. https://slate.com/news-and-politics/2010/01/how-would-pope-john-paul-ii-have-gone-about-self flagellating.html.

Besse, Jean. "Hermits." *The Catholic Encyclopedia*. Vol. 7. New York: Robert Appleton Company, 1910. https://www.newadvent.org/cathen/07280a.htm.

Biondo, Janet Sugameli. "Local Italian Catholics Have Powerful Connection to Soon-to-Be Canonized Saint." Detroit Catholic. May 12, 2022. https://www.detroitcatholic.com/news/local-italian-catholics-have-powerful-connection-to-soon-to-be-canonized-saint.

Brighenti, Kenneth, James Cafone, Jonathan Toborowsky, and John Trigilio Jr. *Catholicism All-in-One for Dummies*. New York: Wiley, 2019.

Brockhaus, Hannah. "Charles de Foucauld: The Miracle That Paved the Way for His Canonization." Catholic News Agency. May 13, 2022. https://www.catholicnewsagency.com/news/251226/charles-de-foucauld-and-the-miracle-that-paved-the-way-for-his-canonization.

Brown, Peter. *The Cult of the Saints: Its Rise and Function in Latin Christianity*. Chicago: University of Chicago Press, 1981.

Campbell, Thomas. "Asceticism." *The Catholic Encyclopedia*. Vol. 1. New York: Robert Appleton Company, 1907. https://www.newadvent.org/cathen/01767c.htm.

Castleden, Rodney. *The Book of Saints*. London, UK: Quercus, 2006.

"Catechism of the Catholic Church." The Holy See. Accessed November 4, 2022. https://www.vatican.va/archive/ENG0015/__P86.HTM.

"Catholic Church Examines Financial Cost of Sainthood." All Things Considered. NPR. February 23, 2014. https://www.npr.org/2014/02/23/281731768/catholic-church-examines-financial-cost-of-sainthood.

Catholic Online. "St. Victor and Corona—Saints & Angels." Accessed November 9, 2022. https://www.catholic.org/saints/saint.php?saint_id=1968.

"Chapter V: The Arrangement and Ornamentation of Churches for the Celebration of the Eucharist." United States Conference of Catholic Bishops. Accessed September 15, 2022. https://www.usccb.org/prayer-and-worship/the-mass/general-instruction-of-the-roman-missal/girm-chapter-5.

Cheng, Amy. "Pope Francis: Don't Choose Pets over Children as Birthrates Drop." *Washington Post*. January 6, 2022. https://www.washingtonpost.com/world/2022/01/06/pope-francis-pet-children-selfish/.

"Dicastery for the Causes of Saints Profile." The Holy See. Accessed September 26, 2022. https://www.vatican.va/content/romancuria/en/dicasteri/dicastero-cause-santi/profilo.html.

Craughwell, Thomas J. *Saints Behaving Badly: The Cutthroats, Crooks, Trollops, Con Men, and Devil-Worshippers Who Became Saints*. New York: Doubleday, 2006.

Craughwell, Thomas J. *Saints Preserved: An Encyclopedia of Relics*. New York: Image Books, 2011.

Creighton-Jobe, Ronald, Mary Frances Budzik, Michael Kerrigan, and Charles Phillips, eds. *The Complete Illustrated Guide to Catholicism*. New Castle, PA: Hermes House, 2009.

Cruz, Joan Carroll. *The Incorruptibles: A Study of the Incorruption of the Bodies of Various Catholic Saints and Beati*. Charlotte, NC: Tan Books and Publishers, 1977.

Cummings, Kathleen Sprows. *A Saint of Our Own: How the Quest for a Holy Hero Helped Catholics Become American*. Chapel Hill: The University of North Carolina Press, 2021.

Doble, Flora. "Saint Sebastian as a Gay Icon." Art UK. January 20, 2022. https://artuk.org/discover/stories/saint-sebastian-as-a-gay-icon.

Domonoske, Camila. "New Vatican Rules Will Put More Spreadsheets into the Saint-Making Process." The Two Way. NPR. March 10, 2016. https://www.npr.org/sections/thetwo-way/2016/03/10/469927636/new-vatican-rules-will-put-more-spreadsheets-into-the-saint-making-process.

Drape, Joe. *Saint Makers: Inside the Catholic Church and How a War Hero Inspired a Journey of Faith*. New York: Hachette Books, 2022.

Duhigg, Charles. "Is Mother Teresa's Miracle for Real?" *Slate*. October 22, 2003. https://slate.com/news-and-politics/2003/10/how-the-vatican-verifies-miracles.html.

Encyclopedia Britannica. s.v. "Pope." Last updated October 18, 2023. https://www.britannica.com/topic/pope.

Encyclopedia Britannica. s.v. "Roman Catholicism—Baptism." Accessed October 12, 2022. https://www.britannica.com/topic/Roman-Catholicism/Baptism.

Encyclopedia Britannica. s.v. "San Diego." Accessed November 6, 2022. https://www.britannica.com/place/San-Diego-California.

Encyclopedia Britannica. s.v. "Santa Fe." Accessed November 6, 2022. https://www.britannica.com/place/Santa-Fe-New-Mexico.

Encyclopedia Britannica. s.v. "Santa Monica." Accessed November 6, 2022. https://www.britannica.com/place/Santa-Monica.

Encyclopedia.com. s.v. "Canonization of Saints (History and Procedure)." Accessed August 26, 2022. https://www.encyclopedia.com/religion/encyclopedias-almanacs-transcripts-and-maps/canonization-saints-history-and-procedure.

Evans, Brandon A. "Cause for Canonization of Bishop Bruté Closer to Official Opening." Archdiocese of Indianapolis. April 22, 2005. https://www.archindy.org/criterion/local/causes/brute2.htm.

Falcone, Alissa. "The Story of the World's Wealthiest Nun." Drexel News. December 2, 2014. http://drexel.edu/news/archive/2014/December/Katharine-Drexel-Book.

Fallon, Claire. "All the Murdered Virgin Saints and Me." *HuffPost*. November 21, 2018. https://www.huffpost.com/entry/virgin-martyr-saints-catholic-rape_n_5bdb3250e4b01abe6a1c47c4.

Flock, Elizabeth. "Pope John Paul II Supposedly Performed Both Miracles after Death." *U.S. News*. July 5, 2013. https://www.usnews.com/news/articles/2013/07/05/pope-john-paul-ii-supposedly-performed-both-miracles-after-death.

Florentin, Louisa. "Blessed Maria Domenica Mantovani: A Mother of 'All Things for All People.'" Salt + Light Media. May 6, 2022. https://slmedia.org/blog/blessed-maria-domenica-mantovani-a-mother-of-all-things-for-all-people.

Foley, Michael P. *Drinking with Your Patron Saints: The Sinner's Guide to Honoring Namesakes and Protectors*. Washington, DC: Regnery History, 2020.

Freze, Michael. *The Cause of Canonization: How Saints Become Saints!* Self-published, Createspace, 2016.

Gallagher, Delia, Daniel Burke, and James Masters. "Vatican Issues Guidelines on Cremation, Says No to Scattering Ashes." CNN. October 25, 2016. https://www.cnn.com/2016/10/25/europe/cremation-vatican-scattering/index.html.

Gladstone, Rick. "Dogs in Heaven? Pope Francis Leaves Pearly Gates Open." *New York Times*. December 12, 2014. https://www.nytimes.com/2014/12/12/world/europe/dogs-in-heaven-pope-leaves-pearly-gate-open-.html.

Glatz, Carol. "Vatican Statistics Show Continued Growth in Number of Catholics Worldwide." *National Catholic Reporter*. March 26, 2021. https://www.ncronline.org/vatican/vatican-statistics-show-continued-growth-number-catholics-worldwide.

Glicksman, Kristina. "Blessed Luigi Maria Palazzolo: Friend of the Poor and Abandoned." Salt + Light Media. May 4, 2022. https://slmedia.org/blog/blessed-luigi-maria-palazzolo-friend-of-the-poor-and-abandoned.

Glicksman, Kristina. "Mother Maria Francesca Rubatto: Uruguay's First Canonized Saint." Salt + Light Media. May 3, 2022. https://slmedia.org/blog/mother-maria-francesca-rubatto-uruguays-first-canonized-saint.

Gribble, Richard. "How Does the Canonization Process Work?" *Simply Catholic*. February 18, 2022. https://www.simplycatholic.com/saints-in-the-christian-tradition/.

Guiley, Rosemary. *The Encyclopedia of Saints*. New York: Checkmark Books, 2001.

"Halo." Christian Symbology. Accessed September 15, 2022. https://www.christiansymbols.net/halo.html.

Head, Thomas. *The Cult of the Saints and Their Relics*. New York: Hunter College and the Graduate Center, 1999.

Heinlein, Michael R., ed. *Black Catholics on the Road to Sainthood*. Huntington, IN: Our Sunday Visitor, 2021.

"History." National Shrine of St. Dymphna. Accessed October 21, 2022. https://natlshrinestdymphna.org/site/?page_id=11.

Hoffner, Helen, and Deidre Folley. *Catholic Traditions & Treasures: An Illustrated Encyclopedia*. Bedford, NH: Sophia Institute Press, 2018.

"Holy Cross." Tanana Chiefs Conference. Accessed November 6, 2022. https://www.tananachiefs.org/about/communities/holy-cross/.

Hooper, John. "It's a Dog's Afterlife: Pope Francis Hints That Animals Go to Heaven." *Guardian*. November 27, 2014. https://www.theguardian.com/world/2014/nov/27/pope-francis-hints-animals-heaven.

"How St. Augustine Got Its Name." Visit St. Augustine. Accessed August 1, 2020. https://www.visitstaugustine.com/article/how-st-augustine-got-its-name.

"Il Dicastero." Dicastero delle Cause dei Santi. Accessed August 8, 2022. http://www.causesanti.va/it/dicastero-delle-cause-dei-santi.html.

"Instruction 'Relics in the Church: Authenticity and Conservation.'" Congregation for the Causes of Saints. The Holy See. Accessed November 13, 2022. https://www.vatican.va/roman_curia/congregations/csaints/documents/rc_con_csaints_doc_20171208_istruzione-reliquie_en.html#PART_I_.

John Paul II. "Divinus Perfectionis Magister." Apostolic Constitutions. The Holy See. Accessed

September 18, 2022. https://www.vatican.va/content/john-paul-ii/en/apost_constitutions/documents/hf_jp-ii_apc_25011983_divinus-perfectionis-magister.html.

"John XXIII Canonized for Sainthood by Pope Francis Who Bypasses Need for Second Miracle." *HuffPost*. July 5, 2013. https://www.huffpost.com/entry/-john-xxiii-sainthood_n_3549910.

John XXIII. "Mater et Magistra." The Holy See. Accessed October 28, 2022. https://www.vatican.va/content/john-xxiii/en/encyclicals/documents/hf_j-xxiii_enc_15051961_mater.html.

Johnson, Stephen. "12 World Leaders with Even Shorter Reigns than Liz Truss." Lifehacker. October 26, 2022. https://lifehacker.com/12-world-leaders-with-even-shorter-reigns-than-liz-trus-1849702739.

Kennedy, Merrit. "Pope Francis Announces New Path to Sainthood." NPR. July 11, 2017. https://www.npr.org/sections/thetwo-way/2017/07/11/536689074/pope-francis-announces-new-path-to-sainthood.

La Vella, Giancarlo. "Looking for Saints: The 'Most Successful' Types of Human Beings." Vatican News. Updated July 1, 2022. https://www.vaticannews.va/en/vatican-city/news/2021-05/dicastery-project-congregation-causes-of-saints-vatican.html.

Landry, Roger. "Blessed Justin Russolillo: A Faithful Foreman for the Lord of the Harvest." *National Catholic Register*. May 13, 2022. https://www.ncregister.com/blog/blessed-justin-russolillo-a-faithful-foreman-for-the-lord-of-the-harvest.

Lisa Bramen. "Lussekatter and Cuccia for St. Lucy's Day." *Smithsonian* magazine. December 10, 2010. https://www.smithsonianmag.com/arts-culture/lussekatter-and-cuccia-for-st-lucys-day-26001669/.

Mares, Courtney. "Pope Francis Approves Miracle Attributed to a French Nun Who Will Be Made a Saint." Catholic News Agency. December 13, 2021. https://www.catholicnewsagency.com/news/249868/pope-francis-approves-miracle-attributed-to-a-french-nun-who-will-be-made-a-saint.

Martinez, Jeremiah. "How Did Sacramento and Surrounding Counties Get Their Names?" Fox40. July 30, 2022. https://fox40.com/news/local-news/sacramento-county-california-names/.

"Martyrs of Korea." Catholic Online. Accessed September 17, 2022. https://www.catholic.org/saints/saint.php?saint_id=4774.

Maura, JP. "Thanos' Infinity Gauntlet Looks Eerily Similar to a Catholic Relic." Aleteia. May 1, 2019. https://aleteia.org/2019/05/01/thanos-infinity-gauntlet-looks-eerily-similar-to-a-catholic-relic/.

McCloskey, Pat. "Red, White, and Green Martyrs?" Franciscan Media. May 23, 2020. https://www.franciscanmedia.org/ask-a-franciscan/red-white-and-green-martyrs.

"Medieval Sourcebook: Stephen de Bourbon (d. 1262): De Superstitione: On St. Guinefort." Internet Medieval Source Book. Accessed August 11, 2022. https://sourcebooks.fordham.edu/source/guinefort.asp.

Neuman, Scott. "15-Year-Old Computer Whiz Who Died in 2006 Could Become 1st Millennial Catholic Saint." NPR. October 12, 2020. https://www.npr.org/2020/10/12/923040054/15-year-old-computer-whiz-who-died-in-2006-could-become-first-millennial-saint.

"New Laws for the Causes of Saints." Congregation for the Causes of Saints. The Holy See. Accessed July 8, 2022. https://www.vatican.va/roman_curia/congregations/csaints/documents/rc_con_csaints_doc_07021983_norme_en.html.

"New Procedures in the Rite of Beatification." Congregation for the Causes of Saints. The Holy See. Accessed December 19, 2022. https://www.vatican.va/roman_curia/congregations/csaints/documents/rc_con_csaints_doc_20050929_saraiva-martins-beatif_en.html.

Norwich, John Julius. *Absolute Monarchs: A History of the Papacy*. New York: Random House, 2011.

"Not Just Red Anymore: The Colors of Martyrdom." The Compass, January 23, 2009. https://www.thecompassnews.org/2009/01/not-just-red-anymore-the-colors-of-martyrdom/.

Nuzzi, Gianluigi. *Merchants in the Temple: Inside Pope Francis's Secret Battle against Corruption in the Vatican*. New York: Henry Holt and Company, 2015.

O'Connell, Gerard. "Pope Francis Brings New Transparency to the Cost of Making Saints." *America*. March 23, 2016. https://www.americamagazine.org/issue/money-and-saint-making.

"Penances." St. John Vianney, Parish Priest of Ars. Accessed October 25, 2022. https://digilander.libero.it/raxdi/ars/inglese/penitenze.htm.

Pool, Bob. "City of Angels' First Name Still Bedevils Historians." *Los Angeles Times*. March 26, 2005. https://www.latimes.com/archives/la-xpm-2005-mar-26-me-name26-story.html.

Prichep, Deena. "Thank the Patron Saint of Bakers for This Cake Today." NPR. May 16, 2012. https://www.npr.org/sections/thesalt/2012/05/16/152818748/thank-the-patron-saint-of-bakers-for-this-cake-today.

"Proof of Miracles Is Elusive // John Paul II." *Tampa Bay Times*. Updated June 20, 2006. https://www.tampabay.com/archive/2003/10/19/proof-of-miracles-is-elusive-john-paul-ii/.

Pullella, Philip. "How Much Is That Halo? Pope Imposes Checks on Costs of Making Saints." Reuters. March 10, 2016. https://www.reuters.com/article/us-pope-saints-idUSKCN0WC1WH.

"Relic Chapel." Maria Stein Shrine of the Holy Relics. Accessed July 12, 2022. https://mariasteinshrine.org/relic-chapel.

Reese, Thomas. "Reformed Canonization Rite Returns." *National Catholic Reporter*. November 23, 2014. https://www.ncronline.org/blogs/ncr-today/reformed-canonization-rite-returns.

Ross, Scott. "New Pope Takes on 8 Official Titles, But Pope's Not One." NBC Washington. Updated March 13, 2013. https://www.nbcwashington.com/news/national-international/pope-titles/1937813/.

"Saint to Be: The Two Miracles of Charles de Foucauld." *Latin Patriarchate of Jerusalem*. Accessed September 13, 2022. https://www.lpj.org/archives/saint-to-be-the-two-miracles-of-charles-de-foucauld.html.

"Saints." United States Conference of Catholic Bishops. Accessed July 30, 2022. https://www.usccb.org/offices/public-affairs/saints.

"Saints and Blesseds of the Catholic Church by Country." GCatholic.org. Accessed September 18, 2022. http://www.gcatholic.org/saints/countries.htm.

"San Diego (St. Didacus)." The Roman Catholic Diocese of San Diego. Accessed November 5, 2022. https://sdcatholic.org/bishops/saint-didacus/.

Scaraffia, Lucetta. "The Equivalent Canonization of Hildegard of Bingen." Eternal Word Television Network. May 16, 2012. https://www.ewtn.com/catholicism/library/equivalent-canonization-of-hildegard-of-bingen-5452.

Simply Catholic Staff. "What Happens at a Canonization?" Simply Catholic. Accessed March 11, 2022. https://www.simplycatholic.com/what-happens-at-a-canonization/.

Smith, Kyle. *Cult of the Dead: A Brief History of Christianity*. Berkeley: University of California Press, 2022.

"St. Agatha, Virgin and Mother." Vatican News. Accessed December 18, 2022. https://www.vaticannews.va/en/saints/02/05/st--agata--virgin-and-martyr.html.

"St. Anthony's Tongue." Atlas Obscura. Accessed August 17, 2022. http://www.atlasobscura.com/places/st-anthonys-tongue.

"St. Etheldreda." Ely Cathedral. Accessed July 22, 2022. https://www.elycathedral.org/about/history-heritage/st-etheldreda.

Tapp, Tom. "Marvel Unveils Real-Life Infinity Gauntlet with Precious Gems Reportedly Worth $25 Million." *Deadline*. July 23, 2022. https://deadline.com/2022/07/real-life-infinity-gauntlet-gems-25-million-dollars-1235075567/.

"The Chair of Saint Peter the Apostle." Catholic Exchange. February 22, 2023. https://catholicexchange.com/the-chair-of-peter/.

"The History of Canonization." Eternal Word Television Network. Accessed October 17, 2022. https://www.ewtn.com/catholicism/library/history-of-canonization-13746.

The Metropolitan Museum of Art. "Bascinet." TheMet. Accessed July 13, 2022. https://www.metmuseum.org/art/collection/search/21988.

The New American Bible. Wichita, KS: Fireside. 1996–1997 ed.

"The Process of Beatification and Canonization." Eternal Word Television Network. Accessed July 8, 2022. https://www.ewtn.com/catholicism/library/process-of-beatification-and-canonization-13747.

"The Tradition of the Vasilopita (with Recipe)." Antiochian Orthodox Christian Archdiocese of North America. Accessed November 21, 2022. http://ww1.antiochian.org/node/18684.

"Vatican Uses Science to Verify Miracles." *Daily Press*. October 20, 2003. https://www.dailypress.com/news/dp-xpm-20031020-2003-10-20-0310200014-story.html.

Vidmar, John. *The Catholic Church through the Ages: A History*, 2nd ed. Mahwah, NJ: Paulist Press, 2014.

"Watch the Updated Video, Link Below—Bernini, Ecstasy of Saint Teresa." Smarthistory. August 21, 2012. YouTube video, 7:32. www.youtube.com/watch?v=RKcJvjP9zgY&t=305s.

"What Happens at Baptism?" *Loyola Press*. Accessed October 14, 2022. https://www.loyolapress.com/catholic-resources/sacraments/baptism/what-happens-at-baptism/.

"Why Is St. Louis Named after a French King Who Was Born 800 Years Ago?" St. Louis Local Public Radio. April 22, 2014. https://news.stlpublicradio.org/show/st-louis-on-the-air/2014-04-22/why-is-st-louis-named-after-a-french-king-who-was-born-800-years-ago.

Wilkinson, Rachel. "A Pittsburgh Church Holds the Greatest Collection of Relics Outside of the Vatican." *Smithsonian* magazine. July 2017. https://www.smithsonianmag.com/arts-culture/pittsburgh-church-greatest-collection-relics-outside-vatican-180963680/.

Wilson, Matthew. *The Halo: A Symbol That Spread around the World*. BBC. June 24, 2021. https://www.bbc.com/culture/article/20210623-the-halo-a-symbol-that-spread-around-the-world.

Winfield, Nicole. "Pope Rallies from Knee Pain to Proclaim 10 New Saints." NBC Boston. Updated

May 15, 2022. https://www.nbcboston.com/news/national-international/pope-francis-rallies-knee-pain-proclaims-10-new-catholic-saints/2720683/. Accessed September 13, 2022.

Wooden, Cindy. "Faith, Fortitude, Martyrdom, Miracles: Pope Will Recognize 10 New Saints." Detroit Catholic. May 10, 2022. https://www.detroitcatholic.com/news/faith-fortitude-martyrdom-miracles-pope-will-recognize-10-new-saints.

Woodward, Kenneth L. *Making Saints: How the Catholic Church Determines Who Becomes a Saint, Who Doesn't, and Why*. New York: Simon & Schuster, 1996.

"Zeppole Di San Giuseppe: A Traditional Neapolitan Pastry Creation." Visit Naples. Accessed September 30, 2022. https://www.visitnaples.eu/en/neapolitanity/flavours-of-naples/zeppole-di-san-giuseppe-a-traditional-neapolitan-pastry-creation.

Photo Attributions

Page 19. Caravaggio, Michelangelo Merisi da. *Judith Beheading Holofernes*. c. 1599. Oil on Canvas, 57 × 77" (145 x 195 cm). National Gallery of Ancient Art, Italy. https://commons.wikimedia.org/wiki/File:Judith_Beheading_Holofernes_-_Caravaggio.jpg.

Page 35. Beck, Leonhard. *Saint Ulrich of Augsburg*. c. 1510. Oil on panel, 46.6 × 19.2" (118.5 × 49 cm). Bildindex der Kunst und Architektur. https://commons.wikimedia.org/wiki/File:Leonhard_Beck_-_Heiliger_Ulrich_(Veste_Coburg).jpg.

Page 42. Unknown. *The Ladder of Divine Ascent*. Twelfth century. Icon. St. Catherine Monastery. Photographed by Michel Bakni. https://commons.wikimedia.org/wiki/File:The_Ladder_of_Divine_Ascent_Monastery_of_St_Catherine_Sinai_12th_century.jpg.

Page 46. Zurbarán, Francisco de. *Saint Apollonia*. 1636. Oil on canvas, 44.4 × 25.9" (113 × 66 cm). Louvre Museum. https://commons.wikimedia.org/wiki/File:Francisco_de_Zurbar%C3%A1n_035.jpg.

Page 51. Tiepolo, Gionvanni Battista. *St. Catherine of Siena*. c. 1746. Oil on canvas, 27.6 × 20.5" (70 × 52 cm). Kunsthistorisches Museum, Vienna. https://commons.wikimedia.org/wiki/File:Giovanni_Battista_Tiepolo_096.jpg.

Page 52, 63. Zurbarán, Francisco de. *Saint Agathe*. c. 1630–1633. Oil on canvas, 50 × 23.6" (27 × 60 cm). Fabre Museum. https://en.wikipedia.org/wiki/Agatha_of_Sicily#/media/File:Santa_Agueda_-_Zurbar%C3%A1n_(detalle).png.

Page 52. Mortellaro, Stefano. *Minnuzze Di Sant'aita*. 2005. Photograph. Flickr. https://commons.wikimedia.org/wiki/File:Minnuzze_di_sant%27aita.jpg.

Page 55. Wolgemut, Michael, and Wilhelm Pleydenwurff. *Portrait of Alexius von Edessa*. c. 1493. Illustration. *Nuremberg Chronicle*. https://commons.wikimedia.org/wiki/File:Schedel_Weltchronik_CXXXV_Alexius-von-Edessa.jpg.

Page 58. Gómez, Vincente Salvador. *Aparición de la Virgen a San Alberto Magno*. c. 1660. Oil on canvas, 51.9 × 39.3" (132 × 100 cm). Museum of Fine Arts of Valencia. https://commons.wikimedia.org/wiki/File:Vicente_salvador_gomez-san_alberto.jpg.

Page 65. Kalteysen, Wilhelm. *Saint Barbara Altarpiece*. 1447. Tempera and gold on spruce wood, 70.9 × 102.3" (203 × 260 cm). National Museum in Warsaw. https://sw.wikipedia.org/wiki/Faili:Wilhelm_Kalteysen_-_Saint_Barbara_Altarpiece_-_Google_Art_Project.jpg.

Page 66. Beccafumi, Domenico di Pace. *Saint Lucy*. 1521. Oil on panel. Pinacoteca Nazionale. https ://commons.wikimedia.org/wiki/File:Saint_Lucy_by_Domenico_di_Pace_Beccafumi.jpg.

Page 69. Unknown. Mosaic of St. Basil the Great. Eleventh century. Kiev Hagia Sophia. https:// commons.wikimedia.org/wiki/File:Basil_of_Caesarea.jpg June 23, 2023.

Page 72. Pacheco, Francisco. *San Luis, rey de Francia*. c. 1610. Oil on panel, 22 × 11.4" (56 × 29 cm). Museo de Bellas Artes de Sevilla. https://commons.wikimedia.org/wiki/File:San_Luis,_rey _de_Francia,_de_Francisco_Pacheco_(Museo_de_Bellas_Artes_de_Sevilla).jpg.

Page 75. Unknown. *Saint Catherine Converting the Scholars*. c. 1480. Oil on panel, 8 × 5.9" (20.5 × 15.2 cm). Walters Art Museum. https://commons.wikimedia.org/wiki/File:Flemish_-_Saint _Catherine_Converting_the_Scholars_-_Walters_372487.jpg.

Page 76. Unknown. Mosiac detail of Pope John VII. c. 705–06 CE. Vatican Museums. https:// aleteia.org/2019/10/27/there-was-a-time-in-which-square-halos-were-a-thing-in-christian -art/.

Page 77. Angelico, Fra. *The Dominican Blessed: Outer Right Pilaster Panel*. c. 1423–4. Egg tempera on wood, 12.5 × 8.6" (31.8 × 21.9 cm). The National Gallery. https://www.nationalgallery.org .uk/paintings/fra-angelico-the-dominican-blessed-1.

Page 89. Bruni, Nikolai Alexandrovich. *Saint Olga, Princess of Kiev, Second Half of the 19th Century*. 1901. State Russian Museum, St. Petersburg. https://commons.wikimedia.org/wiki /File:Olga_of_Kiev.gif.

Page 92. Bouts, Dieric. *Saint Christopher and the Infant Christ*. c. 1479–83. Oil on oak panel, 14.5 × 9.6" (37 × 24.5 cm). Metropolitan Museum of Art. https://commons.wikimedia.org/wiki /File:Saint_Christopher_and_the_Infant_Christ_MET_LC-1975_1_115-001.jpg.

Page 95. Champaigne, Philippe de. *Saint Augustine*. c. 1645–50. Oil on canvas, 30.9 × 24.4" (78.7 × 62.2 cm). Los Angeles County Museum of Art. https://commons.wikimedia.org/wiki/File :Saint_Augustine_by_Philippe_de_Champaigne.jpg.

Page 97. Correa de Vivar, Juan. *Maritirio de San Andrés*. c. 1540–1545. Oil on panel, 38.7 × 27.7" (98.5 × 70.5 cm). Museo del Prado. https://en.wikipedia.org/wiki/File:Martirio_de_San_Andr %C3%A9s,_por_Juan_Correa_de_Vivar.jpg.

Page 99. Raphael. *Granduca Madonna*. c.1505–1506. Oil on panel, 33.2 × 22" (84.4 × 55.9 cm). Galleria Palatina, Florence. https://commons.wikimedia.org/wiki/File:Madona_del_gran _duque,_por_Rafael.jpg.

Page 100. Pontormo, Jacopo. *Saint Quentin*. c. 1517–1518. Oil on panel, 64.1 × 40.5" (163 × 103 cm). Museo Civico di Sansepolcro. https://commons.wikimedia.org/wiki/File:Jacopo_Pontormo _043.jpg.

Page 100. Raphael. *St. Michael*. c.1504–1505. Fresco, 16.4 × 25.2" (500 × 770 cm). Louvre Museum. https://commons.wikimedia.org/wiki/File:St_Michael_Raphael.jpg.

Page 101. Balaca, Eduardo. *Santa Teresa de Jesús*. c. 1877. Oil on canvas, 39.7 × 29.9" (101 × 76 cm). Museo del Prado. https://commons.wikimedia.org/wiki/File:Santa_Teresa_de_Jes%C3 %BAs_(Museo_del_Prado).jpg.

Page 101. Ingres, Jean-August-Dominique. *Joan of Arc at the Coronation of Charles VII in Reims Cathedral*. c. 1854. 94.4 × 70" (240 × 178 cm). The Louvre. https://www.britannica.com /biography/Saint-Joan-of-Arc#/media/1/304220/51269.

Page 108. Unknown. Photograph of Saint Katherine Drexel. c. 1910–1920. Photograph. https://commons.wikimedia.org/wiki/File:Katharine_Drexel.jpg.

Page 116. Coello, Claudio. *Santa Rosa de Lima*. 1683. Oil on canvas. 94.4 × 62.9" (240 × 160 cm). Museo del Prado. https://commons.wikimedia.org/wiki/File:Sta_Rosa_de_Lima_por_Claudio_Coello.jpg.

Page 118. Paola, Giovanni di. *Der hl. Fabian und der hl. Sebastian*. c. 1475. Egg tempera on wood, 33.3 × 21.5" (84.5 × 54.5 cm). National Gallery. https://commons.wikimedia.org/wiki/File:Saint_Fabian1.jpg.

Page 124. Unknown. Icon of Saint Simeon Stylites the Elder. c. 1664. Musée d'Art et d'Histoire de Genève. https://commons.wikimedia.org/wiki/File:Saint_Simeon_Stylites_the_Elder_(1664_icon).jpg.

Page 142. Unknown. Illustration from Hildegard von Bingen's *Scivias*. c. 1151. Illuminated manuscript. *Scivias*. https://commons.wikimedia.org/wiki/File:Hildegard_von_Bingen.jpg.

Page 143. Weidemeyer-Worpswede, Carl. *Saint Francis Instructs the Wolf*. 1911. Engraving. https://commons.wikimedia.org/wiki/File:Francis_wolf.JPG.

Page 144. Mazzanti, Ludovico. *S. Giuseppe da Copertino si Eleva in volo alla vista della Basilica di Loreto*. 1767. Painting. Church of Saint Joseph of Cupertino. https://commons.wikimedia.org/wiki/File:San_Giuseppe_da_Copertino_si_eleva_in_volo_alla_vista_della_Basilica_di_Loreto.jpg.

Page 151. Unknown. Saint Chad. c. 1920. Stained glass. Holy Cross Monastery, West Park, New York. https://commons.wikimedia.org/wiki/File:Saint_Chad.jpg.

Page 161. Cerretani, Giovanni. *The Head of St. Catherine of Siena Exposed in the Basilica of San Domenica, Siena, During a Procession*. https://commons.wikimedia.org/wiki/File:Head_of_Saint_Catherine_of_Siena.jpg.

Page 166. Bourdichon, Jean. Illustration from *Horae ad usum Parisiensem* or "Book of Hours of Charles VIII." c. 1475–1500. Illuminated manuscript. Bibliothèque nationale de France. https://commons.wikimedia.org/wiki/File:StDenis.jpg.

ABOUT THE AUTHOR

Photo by Alex Schaefer

Kate Sidley is a comedy writer and performer originally from Cleveland, Ohio. She writes for *The Late Show with Stephen Colbert*, and her work can be seen in the *New Yorker*, *McSweeney's*, and *Reductress*. Kate has multiple Emmy nominations, a Peabody Award, a Writers Guild Award, and, thanks to her years of Catholic school, a visceral aversion to plaid wool skirts. She lives in New York with her husband, Joe, and their two awesome kids.